Henry Norman Hudson

A Chaplain's Campaign With Gen. Butler

Henry Norman Hudson

A Chaplain's Campaign With Gen. Butler

ISBN/EAN: 9783337424176

Printed in Europe, USA, Canada, Australia, Japan

Cover: Foto ©Andreas Hilbeck / pixelio.de

More available books at **www.hansebooks.com**

A CHAPLAIN'S

CAMPAIGN WITH GEN. BUTLER.

⸺⬦⸺

New-York:

PRINTED FOR THE AUTHOR.

—

1865.

Campaign with Gen. Butler.

New-York:
PRINTED FOR THE AUTHOR.

—

1865.

A CHAPLAIN'S

CAMPAIGN WITH GENERAL BUTLER.

NEW-YORK, Jan. 4, 1865.

To Major-General B. F. Butler, Commanding Department of Virginia and North-Carolina:

GENERAL : Under date of Sept. 26th, 1864, I wrote out and sent to you a pretty full Statement of my case, being advised thereto by Colonel Edward W. Serrell, speaking, as I understood him, at your instance or request. I now beg leave to lay before you another statement, and to invite your special attention to it. The main particulars of this latter statement were noted down by me a few days after their occurrence, so that I feel pretty confident I have them about right. And I think it may do you good to reproduce them to you, and to give you a fair opportunity to ruminate them at your leisure.

For the better understanding of the matter in hand, I will preface it with a few items from my Statement of Sept. 26th.

Before going to the seat of war, which was in February, 1862, I entered into an engagement with Parke Godwin, Esq., of the New-York *Evening Post*, to write for that paper. While in the Department of the South under Generals Hunter, Mitchel, and Gillmore, I made that engagement known to them, and had occasional interviews with them, or their representatives, in reference to it. Soon after landing at Bermuda Hundred, last May, I went to your Provost-Marshal, told him who I was, informed him of my engagement with Mr. Godwin, and asked if there were any restrictions on newspaper correspondence, or any regulations concerning it. I understood him to say there were none, and so thought I should not be wrong in continuing to write for the paper.

My articles written for publication in the *Evening Post* were signed "Loyalty," and published with that signature. Besides these, I often wrote private letters to Mr. Godwin, which were not meant to be published, and were not published.

Soon after your grand defeat up on Proctor's Creek, near Drury's Bluff, I wrote a private letter to Mr. Godwin, giving what I believed to be a fair and truthful account of that adventure. I put the matter in that form, partly because I had some doubt as to the propriety of setting it directly before the public. Most of the letter appeared in the *Evening Post* of May 24th. As a private letter, it was signed with my own name, but was printed without any signature, the editor introducing it with a sort of voucher for its authenticity.

On the 29th of May, General Gillmore ordered me to New-York on special duty ; which duty, he said, was to superintend the printing of some official matter to be published by Mr. Van Nostrand. The General, on giving me the order, said he would send to the publisher for me particular instructions in what I was to do. As I had, the night before, learned by telegraph, that my son William was very dangerously ill, the General gave me at the same time permission to go to my family in Massachusetts.

My son died the first week in June ; and his mother, broken down with grief and care, was sick nearly all the Summer; so much so, that at one time she was hardly expected to live. I was also very much out of health myself, from the effects of a bilious intermittent fever, contracted while on duty in South-Carolina. About the middle of June, I wrote to Mr. Van Nostrand, to know if any instructions had come for me from General Gillmore. He replied that none had come, and if any should come he would notify me at once. Not very long after this, General Gillmore was relieved of his command of the Tenth Army Corps, so that I was no longer subject to his order.

Early in July, I was in New-York, and there received an

order from you remanding me to my regiment. As our Colonel was then in the city, I called on him to know where I should report. He replied, in effect, that he could not tell, the regiment being so scattered that he hardly knew where the headquarters were: " I do not know," said he, " but I am as much the headquarters as anywhere." The next day, I learned that my wife was a good deal worse; and, being somewhat perplexed as to my duty, I ventured to return to my family, where I was soon after so prostrated with illness as to be unable to travel. Owing to these causes, I was delayed from day to day, till I became discouraged, and resolved to offer my resignation. Accordingly I went to New-York, and on the first of September handed my resignation to Colonel Serrell, who said he would forward it to you, and that he thought there was no need of my going on to the seat of war.

On the 13th, the Colonel, being still in New-York, as I also was, received a telegram as follows:

" BUTLER'S HEADQUARTERS, Sept. 13, 1864.

" *To Colonel Serrell,* 57 *West Washington Place :*

" Find Chaplain Hudson, of your regiment, who has been ordered to report to his regiment, and has failed to obey the order. Take his parole in writing forthwith to appear at these Headquarters: if he fails to give his parole, have him sent here to me under guard. Your special attention is called to the executing of this order.

(Signed)   " B. F. BUTLER,

         " Major-General."

I had been told you were a vindictive man, but was loth to believe it. This order looked rather threatening indeed ; nevertheless, I gave my parole at once, hastened forward as fast as I could, and " appeared" at your Headquarters on the 19th. As for your words—" if he fails to give his parole, have him sent here to me under guard"—I thought them somewhat brutal in temper and spirit ; for you did not know me personally ; the fact of my being a clergyman ought not to have been with you any presumption against me ; that I had expressed an adverse opinion of your military leadership, was no certain proof of a bad heart in me; and you had no doubt seen my resignation, which had been approved and forwarded to you by my Colonel, and from which you might have learned that I was suffering from "continued and obstinate ill-health, such as to render me unfit for the service." But let that pass : "you must think, look you; that the worm will do his kind."

I had schooled myself well for the meeting with you; was thoroughly armed with the soft answer that turneth away wrath, though not able to turn away your wrath. I did not fear to meet you, Sir, for I supposed you to be so much like other men, that integrity of purpose and a fair cause would be some security with you. In this I was mistaken. In due time I was summoned to an interview with you, which proved to be somewhat long, and rather interesting—at least to me. It was very soon evident that you had called me before you, not for the purpose of hearing me or of learning any thing about me, but merely for the pleasure of browbeating and condemning me. During the interview I observed and studied you intently; of that you may be sure. And, however it may have been before, I *know* you *now*—know you like a book. Indeed, my General, you disappointed me much. You did not appear nearly so well as I had expected; your wits seemed badly out of tune, your whole inner man distempered with unbenevolent passion. You put on airs, indeed you did, that were both mean and silly. Some parts of your performance reminded me of—" Then, a soldier, full of strange oaths, and bearded like the pard, seeking the bubble reputation even in the cannon's mouth." But pardon me : I do not mean to stick upon you the latter part of this description ; for I know of no cannon's mouth that you have ever " sought unto" for reputation or any other bubble. I have seen you ride, and I have heard you swear, though I never saw you doing both at the same time ; but, from what has been told me of your accomplishments in that line, I am moved to suggest that you take this as your motto : "Come, wilt thou see me ride ? and when I am o' horseback I will swear."

Was it because I was a clergyman, Sir, that you thought to storm me into confusion or to strike me dumb' by a coarse exhibition of Butlerism? Did you hope to get your self honour on me by enacting the court-room ruffian at me? and this too in a place where there was no court to protect me against you, or, which was of more importance, to protect you against yourself? where you were at once accuser, attorney, and judge? You proceeded with me throughout just as though you were cross-examining a witness. But your reputation as a low criminal lawyer forbids me to think that you often work through the process so infelicitously as you did on that occasion. I have stood a much sharper cross-examination, Sir; but the lawyer who conducted it was also a gentleman, and therefore I was not disgusted with it.

You first called me to account for having been absent without leave. But I soon explained this, so that you did not seem to think much could be made out of it; not much, that is, save as a handle for working out some other purpose. For, of course, you knew well enough that in the matter of "voluntary absence" custom and usage allow a somewhat wider margin to chaplains than to other officers. And rightly so, inasmuch as chaplains, besides being on rather small pay, have no chance of promotion, but must end in that respect just as they begin; so that ambition, the soldier's virtue, can have no place with them: not to mention that their office does not stand in so close connection with the efficiency of an army as in case of other officers. But, in truth, the circumstances of my case were such as, with all fair-minded men, would go far to excuse any officer in doing as I did.

And so, on my explaining the matter, you presently left this topic, and, with a good deal of unnecessary swaggering and bluster, took me up on that which, as I knew right well all the while, was the real "head and front of my offending." In my letter to Mr. Godwin, already mentioned, I had faulted your generalship in the military operations of last May near Bermuda Hundred. It was for this that you wanted to pinch and wring me. And when I gave you a true account of the matter, this, instead of appeasing your wrath, only seemed to kindle it the more; perhaps because it placed the responsibility of the publication on those whom you could not reach. And here I found you thoroughly in earnest; but I also found that you could not well be in earnest without playing the old bruiser. Your motive, my General, was revenge, too palpably so to admit of any question; indeed, I think you hardly cared to disguise it. And your passion made you unwise, or at least unshrewd; its effect being, I should think, to disedge your wits and dismantle your judgment. At times you waxed pretty decidedly tempestuous, especially when General Gillmore was your theme; repeatedly denouncing him as "a damned scoundrel" and "a liar;"—language which, had you been perfectly cool, I doubt whether even you would have considered exactly "becoming an officer and a gentleman." You seemed, indeed, to be labouring under some malignant hallucination about General Gillmore, as though he were ghosting you, and to have got me strangely mixed up with him therein. At first, you insisted upon it that I had colluded with him, and knowingly lent myself to some naughty designs of his against you. And when I refuted this charge, you then ventilated your inward parts, in effect, and nearly in words, as follows: "As for the great villain in this case, he is beyond my reach, I cannot get at him directly; but, sir, I have got you: he has been making use of you as a poor tool against me; and now, sir, you must serve my turn against him." In proof of my having conspired with him to injure you, you alleged that his ordering me to New-York on special duty was a mere pretext for getting me out of the way, and that I knew it to be so. I assured you that I had no knowledge of the sort; that I had received the order and acted upon it in perfect good faith, honestly believing General Gillmore had some real and legitimate work for me to do in New-York; and in proof of this, I cited the fact of my having written to Mr. Van Nostrand for the instructions which he was to send on for me.

At one stage of the dialogue, when you were trying to make me say something untrue of General Gillmore, my answer not being such as you wanted, you exclaimed, "That's a lie, sir! a damned lie!" which, though polite enough as coming from you, did not strike me as in perfectly good taste.

But I forget : your taste was formed in an atmosphere which I probably cannot appreciate. I have indeed read the Bible some, read Shakespeare some, preached some ; you have— *practised.* That you are a brave man, I am willing to believe ; but I doubt, yea, I doubt very much, whether you would have dared to speak thus to one who was in a condition to resent it. Being a brave man, you ought not, my General, thus to use the dialect of a cowardly ruffian. Remember, I pray you, what it is that defileth a man. And the next time you feel the inspiration of valiantness upon you, don't attempt to make proof of it by assaulting one whose hands are tied.

At another time, on my pleading ignorance in a matter where you did not want me to be ignorant, you exploded nearly thus : " Don't tell me that, sir ; come, sir, you are not a fool ;" and then you added, with, I thought, more of truth than politeness, " You are an ordinary man, sir, an *ordinary* man." This, I believe, was the nearest approach to wit that you were guilty of during the interview. And this was indeed pretty fair, though not nearly so good as I had expected from you. I had it in my mind to reply, "And you, General, are a very extraordinary man ;" but it was not my part to bandy wit or words with you, and so I refrained. On the whole, it was pretty clear that you did not regard me as a gentleman. But were you not something at fault in supposing this to be a good reason for not behaving like a gentleman yourself?

In the course of our interview, you made several Scripture allusions, but I did not think you particularly happy in them ; in truth, you seemed more pedantic than learnedly-wise in your drawings from that source. For instance, you charged me with malice in writing the letter to Mr. Godwin. I assured you otherwise ; that I was indeed very much distressed at the turn things took on the 16th of May ; but that I had all along, both before and after that event, been praising you and standing up for you ; though, to be sure, I thought you would be more useful, and do yourself more credit, in some high administrative position, than where you were. To which you replied nearly thus : " I understand you, sir. You are doubtless familiar with the Scriptures. Was it not Ahab—I think it was Ahab," (you probably meant Joab,) "who said to some one, 'O my brother, my brother!' and at the same time thrust his dagger into him?" "But, General," said I, "how does that apply to me?" whereupon you exclaimed: "You stabbed me in the dark, sir! you stabbed me in the dark! But I have caught you at last; I have you in my power now, sir, and I am going to punish you." Again: I had occasion to remark that our regiment was very much split up and scattered. "Yes," said you; "when the shepherd is away, the sheep will get scattered." I replied: "But, General, in this case the sheep were pretty well scattered before the shepherd went away." Indeed, Sir, I thought you must be rather hard up for matter against me, thus to allege my absence as the occasion of that which you could not but know to have sprung from the necessities of the service.

You accused me of stealing from the Government, in that I had been taking pay without doing any duty. I told you that I had drawn no pay for any of the time since the date of your order remanding me to my regiment; and that I was willing to lose it, if it were judged that I ought to lose it. But, as an offset for this interval of leisure, I then told you that, if I had been in the way to receive pay without working for it, I had also done a good deal of work without getting any pay for it; that I was on duty in New-York and on Staten Island upward of three months before I could get mustered into the service, our officers in command assuring me, meanwhile, that I would be paid; that, during this time, I did some very hard and important work, but had never received any pay, and had given up all hope of getting any. Whereupon you remarked: "That was no credit to you, sir; you expected to be paid." "Of course I did," said I; "for, General, I am a poor man, with a family to support; so that I cannot afford to work without wages, neither would it be right for me to do so." I then told you, further, that while I was thus on duty, word came that our men were suffering dreadfully for want of rubber blankets, and an earnest appeal was made to me to procure them relief. That this was for me a very hard undertaking, but I set right about it, and did not pause till it was done. That, after working with all my might for many days, I at last engaged some dealers to furnish the blankets, on my undertaking to pay for them when the men should be paid. That, accordingly, I gave my written obligation in the sum of $756.25, and thus got the men supplied; the blankets being put to them for precisely what they were put to me. That, owing to some misunderstanding, it was a long time before the men were paid; and when at length a payment was made, some had died, others had been discharged for disability, and the regiment, moreover, was so scattered that I could not get at them. That for two years I used my best diligence in collecting the money, and still was more than $150 out of pocket on that score. And that all this extra-official work was done purely out of kindness to the men and concern for the good of the service. I told you this in all honesty and simplicity, for I still supposed you to be a man. And I spoke of it, not in the way of complaint, but as a fair argument of integrity and earnestness in the cause. You replied to it all by comparing me to Judas! and, as I did not see the aptness of the comparison, you then observed, that I had doubtless taken care to see myself well paid for bearing the bag in that business. You, my General, you were base enough to say that! And I shall hold you to it.

Once more: The current of our talk led me to assure you that I had had none but friendly feelings towards you, and had wished nothing but good to you; and I stated certain facts in evidence of this: at which you turned upon me your most eloquent look, and went to expressing, with tongue and eyes, the utmost contempt for me and my feelings; in fact, you could hardly find words big enough, or looks black enough, to convey your magnanimous scorn. I was truly shocked, Sir, to see that pure and beautiful face of yours all marred and turned awry by so distortive an effort. "Bless us," thought I, "what if his face should marble in that shape! 'twould be enough to scare all the gods and goddesses from their pedestals." Otherwise, I found no fault with your grim mirth, and I still find none; for I really did not think myself worth your revenge; and my greatest wonder all along has been, that you did not see that I was far too insignificant to justify any such emphatic notice as you were taking of me. Indeed, my General, I must say, you have been hunting rather small game for a man of your size. But I doubted whether even your huge resentment could lift me out of my proper obscurity into any sort of consequence. To be sure, your violence, though unheroical enough, was in some respects rather flattering to me; yet I was not altogether pleased with it.

But I was much struck with the disproportion, or what seemed such, between your scorn of me and your resentment of what I had done. For you spoke with exceeding bitterness of the outrageous abuse that had been poured upon you by the Press all over the country, in consequence of what I had written about you. So, too, on my telling you that I should have resigned long ago, but for the necessity of being at hand to collect the money for the rubber blankets, you exclaimed: " Would to God you had done so, sir! would to God you had never come here!" Perhaps it was my vanity that led me to note these passages, but note them I did. And it really seemed to me that if I had been, as I certainly had not, the guilty cause of defeating your aspirations for the Presidency, you could hardly have been more fluent of railing and bitterness against me. I have indeed been credibly informed since, that you hoped and intrigued for the nomination, first, at Baltimore, and then, failing of that, at Chicago; but I am perfect that you never stood the slightest chance at either place, nor would have done so, though I had spent all the brains and all the ink I ever had, in writing up your generalship.

One passage of our conversation I am sure it will delight you to be reminded of. I told you, and truly, that I had often, on hearing you assailed, defended you, and upheld you to be a just and kind-hearted man. You replied that you meant to be just, but, as for kind-heartedness, you spurned the imputation; that you were not kind-hearted, and you scorned to be thought so: it was too like the Yankee phrase "clever fellow," as applied to one rather weak in the upper storey. To which I answered, that I had used the word in a good sense; and that I had found kindness of heart to be of some use among the soldiers. I noticed that, at the hearing of this, your countenance fell somewhat, thus slightly indicating that you wanted much to be popular with the soldiers, and that you were sensible you were not so.

I spoke then as I thought, but I now understand you better. And I acquit you of being kind-hearted : whatever may be your deserts, you clearly deserve no such imputation as that. It has been said that against stupidity the gods themselves are powerless. And so I admit that against the notes of compassion you have the strength of an ox, the firmness of a bear. Certainly my experience of you failed to discover the slightest stirring of a humane or generous chord in your bosom : touch you where I might, I still found you as hard as a flint ; and as your hardness is that of burnt clay, and not of any wintry congelation, of course no warmth can damage it ; it is sun-proof and sky-proof : whether it is proof against all other forces, will be better seen when " even-handed justice commends the ingredients of your poisoned chalice to your own lips." If you are covetous of such honour, take it, for it is yours. Yet I remember, General Sherman, in rehearsing the noble traits of his beloved McPherson, that great young soldier—" the garland of the war "—O, too soon withered!—mentions kindness of heart as among the noblest. But then General Sherman, like his fallen brother, the theme of his praise, is framed of other stuff than you ; being indeed as different from you in this respect as he is in warlike achievement.

And I shall henceforth be careful, withal, how I accuse you of being just ; I have tasted your vindictiveness too much to repeat that mistake. It is certain, moreover, that a man without kindness of heart cannot be just ; for in the nature of things such a man is all compact of selfishness, which is not the complexion of justice ; and it is not in him to know the power or respect the order of so high and sacred a thing, however he may counterfeit the forms and language thereof.

> " Where pity's held intrusive, or turned out,
>   There wisdom will not enter, nor true power,
>   Nor aught that dignifies humanity."

For you must know, my General, that such a man wants the corresponding faculty, the answering sense. So that you might as well discourse the harmonies of justice to a congregation of wild asses, as to him. You, Sir, a just man! and fearing nothing else so much as a bodily hurt or a popular hiss! You a just man! and comprehending no higher force in human affairs than terror and torture! As for your sense or idea of justice, one half of it, I think, must have been in high glee when you juggled and spirited off—whither, O! whither?—that $50,000 of gold in New-Orleans. For the other half, why, when a Shylock or a General Butler talks of justice he means revenge. The smell of blood, sweeter to such than the perfumes of Arabia, is all the sympathy with justice *they* have. And so, in the name and behalf of this august power, " whose seat is the bosom of God, whose voice the harmony of the world," it may with special fitness be said or sung,—*note* it, my General,*—

> " The man that hath no music in himself,
> Nor is not mov'd with concord of sweet sounds,
> Is fit for treasons, stratagems, and spoils;
> The motions of his soul are dull as night,
> And his affections dark as Erebus:
> LET NO SUCH MAN BE TRUSTED."

Out of divers other noteworthy passages in our interview, I shall stay to cite but one more. Referring to my sacred calling, you scoffed at me as a " hypocrite," tossed off a characteristic sneer about my unfitness to be a Christian minister, and then went on, in what sounded very like cant, to lecture me somewhat on the duties of that office. I made no reply to this at the time. But let me assure you now, my General, that I am a clergyman, " in good and regular standing," of the Protestant Episcopal Church. You ought to have known this, for I had preached and ministered a good many times in St. Anne's Church, Lowell, where your own family used to attend. The worthy Rector, Dr. Edson, has known me pretty well for some fifteen years ; probably he has learned as much about me in that time as you could learn during the fifteen minutes we had been together when you emptied your scoffs upon me ; and, if you care to have any information concerning me, I daresay he can give it you. Meanwhile, as regards the

---

* It is well known in the army that General Butler has a strong aversion to music.

matter in question, I demur to your sentence; you are not the proper judge of me in that respect. And a man of your finished proportions should not take upon him to know too much. Be content, I pray you, with your mastership in the art of war, and with the exercise of those unique graces which have made your name a proverb. A bishop's mitre can hardly sit well on the laurelled brows of such a mighty conqueror as the hero of Big Bethel and Proctor's Creek.

Such are a few items of what I experienced at your hand during our interview. You charged me to my face with lying, stealing, fraud, and hypocrisy; you likened me to "Ahab," the traitor-murderer, and to Judas, the traitor-thief; all this, too, when you knew you had me in your power, so that I could not answer your reproaches nor repel your insults. I do not claim to have given the passages in the order of their occurrence, but I do claim to have set them forth with substantial truth. And I think these specimens are a pretty fair average of your behaviour on that occasion. What do you think of them now, my General? Do they not something smack of what Hamlet calls "the insolence of office?" Can you, on cool reflection, can you think it was altogether handsome in you, a Major-General in the army of the United States, thus to insult over a minister of the Gospel, who was in your power, and could not help himself against you? Have you read, and do you remember, the well-known saying of Burke, that "the hatefullest part of tyranny is its contumelies?" For myself, permit me to say, that I cannot think the performance was very creditable to you either as a gentleman, a general, a lawyer, or a theologian. It seems hardly possible that such an achievement should have come by imitation, so I suppose it was purely the result of character. Yet I am persuaded that you did yourself great injustice, and that you would have made a much better showing of your parts, had you deigned to exercise a little of that kind-heartedness which you so pointedly disclaimed. Malice, my General, malice is a potent stultifier.

It is not for me to boast, and I certainly have nothing to boast of in this affair; but I believe I bore your savage insolence tolerably well, considering the inflammable stuff which my friends tell me I am made of. But, whether I bore it like a man or not, I certainly felt it as a man. And I am bold to say, that " if I blushed, it was to see a general want manners." I felt, too, more than once, a pinch of grief, that the higher officers of our army, soldiers and gentlemen as they are, who know what belongs to honour, and civility, and manhood, should have such a low-minded savage consorted with them. But I do not remember to have been once betrayed into any loss of temper or of self-control. Either I was not disconcerted at all, or else I was too much disconcerted to be conscious of it. The interview, I confess, was not perfectly delightful to me ; yet I thought you enjoyed it rather less than I did. The worst part of it was, that you had a lieutenant, a short-hand writer, sitting behind the table, who kept writing all the while, evidently taking us down. I was partly amused, partly vexed, to see this shoulder-strapped underling, the doer of your dirty work, laughing at his master's wit ; but I could not help fearing, for I knew something of your tricks, lest the sequel of all this should be, a Butlerized version of our interview published to the world. I bethought me, however, that in that case my cue also might be,

> " A chield's amang you taking notes,
> And, faith, he'll prent it."

Thus much, my General, for the, to me, memorable interview which I had the honour of holding with you. Your official eloquence did not lead me to expect any very gentle usage from you, and I am bound to say that my usage was far more ungentle than I anticipated. For I still hoped that the laws of the service, which both you and I had solemnly engaged to observe, would be some shield to me. The interview ended (for all such exploits of manhood must have an end) in your placing me in arrest, and handing me over to Captain Watson, commandant of your headquarters guard, who took me to your provost-guard prison, and put me in what he called a magazine tent. This was a tent nearly filled with open boxes of powder and other explosive ammunition, or what seemed such, and among the rest a considerable heap of large shell, charged, as the Captain said, with Greek fire. There was little more than vacant room enough for me to lie down, and that was close beside the heap of loaded shell. The Captain cautioned me not to allow a spark of fire in the tent, and especially not to disturb the shell, lest they should explode and blow me up. What may have been the motive of this warning I cannot say, but it had the effect of the most studied inhumanity : I could not help being in continual apprehension lest some unlucky step of mine should set the shell a-tumbling ; but I found out afterwards that they would bear much rougher handling than I had been led to suppose.

I had never before heard of a magazine tent being set up in any provost-guard prison. I presume the thing had been hit upon by you as a novel engine of torture for certain select victims. It was indeed exquisitely adapted to that end, and was used with exquisite effect in my case. The device was worthy alike of your cunning and your "justice," the counsels of a bad heart and a busy brain being written all over it. If any thing but a guilty conscience can cause a man "on the torture of the mind to lie in restless ecstasy," then such, I think, must have been my condition during the two days spent under this part of your discipline. Very few can imagine what I underwent, and I shall not attempt to describe it. For some time after, as long indeed as I was held within the reach of your claws, I was subject to frequent turns of acute distress, which I called "Butler on the brain." Yet I had been under fire, Sir, and had found myself able to face the dangers of battle with tolerable composure, these being to me mere child's play compared to the choice hell-craft with which you thus made merry at my expense. To have had me ironed, and set to work in your Dutch Gap Canal, though, to be sure, it would have looked much worse, and could scarce have failed to draw upon you an immediate storm of reprobation,. would have distressed me nothing so much as this quiet little arrangement of yours for "punishing" me. Doubtless you perfectly understood all that.

But I must do you the justice to say, that you soon repudiated, apparently, this child of your invention. The magazine tent, after I had occupied it two days, was taken down, and the ammunition removed entirely out of the inclosure. Whether Captain Watson told me what he knew to be false,

2

or whether he was himself deceived, I could not tell; but, from the way the men tossed and banged the shell about in the process of removal, it appeared that the Greek fire, if there was any in them, had gone too fast asleep to be waked up by any ordinary disturbance. Whether the open boxes of powder and other explosive ammunition were also bogus preparations for working out your schemes of torture, I had no means of ascertaining. I was, and I am, very glad, Sir, that you did not keep me any longer in that tent. Yet I am far from suspecting you of any humanity or kindness of heart, in ordering the change. You probably learned that this chosen engine of "justice" was using me up faster than suited your purpose. To have kept me strained up much longer to such a pitch of what may be called nervous ecstasy, would have marked you out too plainly as a deliberate homicide.

When I remonstrated with Captain Watson against being confined in such a place of torment, he replied that such was your order; that is, you ordered him to put me in a tent by myself, and that was the only tent where he could so put me. An average nose will readily smell out the meaning of this. For, of course, such astute tormentors and inquisitors as you, do not commonly perpetrate their crimes and inhumanities without providing beforehand some plausible shifts for eluding the responsibility of their deeds. And so, I make no doubt, you will say, if you have not already said, that you did not order me to be put in that tent, nor even know I was put there. No! you only knew that such an engine of torture stood ready in your prison-pen, and that there was no other unoccupied tent on the ground. This was enough; your order would send me there, as a matter of course; yet not so but that you could ignore the main point, and slip out, if challenged. For such, I have been well assured, is your habitual craft in managing to throw off upon your "agents and base second means" the scandal and blame of your practices. Now, the officer who, under you, had the ordering of my condition was none other than the lieutenant that had been present during our interview. He was your confidential minister, was inward with you, knew your secret mind, understood just what you wanted him to do with me, and was perfectly sure that you would uphold him in what he did, however you might make as though you did not mean it. Like Macbeth in suborning the murder of Banquo, you " required a clearness ;" and to let you stand clear was an understood part of his bargain with you ; your very point being, to get certain things done which you might openly reprove, and secretly reward. With such creatures at your beck, nothing was easier than for you to be left in blissful ignorance of whatever you did not choose to know ; they pleading your orders, and you disclaiming their particular modes of executing them.

That such was your game in my case, appeared in that, as I afterwards learned, until my coming the magazine tent had been most carefully guarded, no prisoner being allowed to look into it, or even to go up to it ; thus showing that it had been set apart for a special use. Well, after all, this kind of moral legerdemain is but an old trick of knaves, to skulk from danger, or to play at hide-and-seek with their fears. If the wit of the thing were as great as the meanness, it might entitle you to a place with Titus Oates. You take a deal of pains, Sir, to cover up your tracks, not observing, meanwhile, that you are seen covering them. I must add, that in cases like mine, your orders are not issued through your adjutant-general's office, but go direct from you to those that are to execute them, so that no public record is made of the proceedings. This method of course arms you, in effect, with full inquisitorial powers, and precludes any check or hindrance to the most tyrannical abuse of power. It scarce need be said, that in the running of this " infernal machine " you do not scruple to realize all the terrible oppressions of which the machine is capable.

To resume my narrative : It was nearly dark when Captain Watson got me housed in the prison. The weather was more than cool ; the ground in the tent was so wet as to be almost muddy ; and there I was left without a rag of a blanket to put under me, or over me, and with nothing to lie on but some barrel-staves, spread out on the ground. I had told the Captain that I was somewhat out of health, and rather old for such hardships, and had asked him to procure me a blanket or two, offering to pay for them. He said he would try to do so ;

I waited, but no blanket came. At last, a corporal of the guard, a very civil, kind-hearted man, named Jones, managed to borrow me a single blanket, which I wrapped round my shoulders, and spent most of the night in walking to and fro over the square of ground in front of my tent, not being allowed to walk beyond it. Even at that I shivered through hour after hour till near morning, when the same gentle corporal took me out to the cook-house, and let me sit by the stove and warm myself. The corporal seemed fearful lest these deeds of charity should come to the knowledge of his officers.

My trunk, containing all my baggage, I had been obliged to leave at the landing-place, some three fourths of a mile from your headquarters. Before going into the prison, I had found means of writing a note to one Lieutenant Davenport, your Assistant Provost-Marshal, and the doer of your dirty work referred to above, describing my trunk, telling him where it was, and requesting him to let me have it, as I greatly needed some of the articles in it. He sent me word the trunk should be brought to me; I expected it, and was disappointed. Had I anticipated any such proceedings, I should have gone first among my old comrades, and engaged some of them to help me through. But I then supposed you to be very different from what you are.

In the morning, a piece of boiled salt fish, a piece of bread rather stale, and a cup of coffee without sugar, were given me. The fish I could not eat, the coffee I could not drink, and so made my breakfast on bread and water; which would have done very well, but that, through cold and want of sleep, and distress of mind, my stomach was so weak and disordered that I could not keep the food down. At that time, I was not allowed to speak with any but officers of the guard; and these were all afraid to do any thing for me, or to let any thing be done; inferring, as they well might, from the usage put upon me, either that I was some desperate criminal, or else that you had strong "personal feelings" against me. Otherwise, I could easily have found ways to supply myself with food. Meanwhile, as I have since learned, you and your creatures were doing what you could to defame and blacken me, hinting that I was a political offender, that I had been caught giving aid and comfort to the enemy, and I know not what other charges, all calculated to set the hearts of men against me, and to shut up the instincts of kindness in those about me.

The second day I applied to Captain Watson again for some blankets, but was told there were none to be had. I also made another appeal to Lieutenant Davenport for my trunk, urging my needs still more earnestly, and he promised again that I should have it. Night came again; my trunk was still kept from me; the corporal had been obliged to return the borrowed blanket; so that I was left without any thing. Rather late in the evening, I managed to get an interview with the Captain, told him my condition, and then addressed him thus: "Captain Watson, I have been under the command of Generals Hunter, Mitchel, and Gillmore, successively, in the Department of the South; while there, I served for a considerable time, voluntarily, as chaplain of the provost-guard quarters; and I remonstrated more than once with the commanding general in behalf of rebel prisoners, who were treated much better than I am here. And I now pledge you my word, sir, that if our present relations should ever be reversed, I will *not* treat you as you are treating me." He replied: "But for your cloth, sir, I should hold myself bound to challenge you for that speech." I got no relief from him, his orders probably not allowing him to give me any; but a fellow-prisoner, Captain Simpson, of a Pennsylvania battery, lent me a blanket and two narrow boards for the night, partly depriving himself. I am grieved to learn that this humane and generous captain has since died. He was a brave and capable man, had done good service, and carried proofs of it in the disease that was undermining his life while I knew him. Why he was thus shut up in your bull-pen I never learned; his experiences there, no doubt, had much to do in causing his death.

On the third day, as I despaired of getting my trunk from Lieutenant Davenport, I addressed a note directly to you, telling you how it was with me, and begging you to let me have my baggage, or at least some part of it, mentioning several articles of which I was in great and pressing need. I was told soon after that you had given, or would give orders to have my trunk brought me. A few hours later, instead of the trunk, came information that the trunk had disappeared, had probably been reshipped down the river, and should be sent for back by the first opportunity. All this appeared to me rather significant. Was I uncharitable in concluding there had been no serious purpose of getting my baggage to me? I know not whether that thing of yours, Lieutenant Davenport, is still near you. If he be, please make my compliments to him : tell him, from me, that if he did not respect me nor my needs, he ought at least to have respected his own word ; and that the man who does not respect his own word must excuse me from respecting it. You may add, that in what I saw of his conduct to other prisoners, he seemed a trifle too ferocious for one so young. Should he keep on at that rate, he will crave some thicker beverage than blood by the time he is as old as you and I are. He knows the whole catechism of profanity by heart, I should think ; and in his recitations he stings it home with a spitefulness worthy of your cherishing. As he has evidently taken you for his great man and his model, it is hardly fair of him to *begin* just like you, only more so.

Such is, in brief, the history of my first three days with you. I can truly say that I would not have treated a dog of yours so ; no, not even if the dog had bit me. Meanwhile, my condition became known to some members of my own regiment, who were quartered near by. They went to work at once for my relief. I saw Captain Eaton, one of our very best officers, told him of my trunk ; he promised to look after it, and *his* promise was kept. He furnished me also with a bunk, a bench, and some blankets, and had me supplied with wholesome and palatable food from his own mess, till I could make arrangements for feeding myself. My mattress and pillow too, which I had put under our Captain Southard when he was brought into the camp mortally wounded, and had left under him when I went North, with instructions that he should have them as long as he might need them,—these were found and returned to me. And in due time two of Captain Eaton's men came, bringing my trunk, and saying they had found it right where I left it, and no signs of its having been

disturbed. My belief then was, and still is, that but for these
friends I should not have seen my trunk again very soon.
You, Sir, did not mean I should have it, so long as any excuse
or pretext could be found or made for keeping it from me.
Captain Watson too, either from shame, or for some other
cause, had another tent put up for me on dry ground. So that
I was now pretty well supplied with what was needful for
bodily comfort. It is well worth remarking, further, that most
of the officers and men of the guard laid aside much of their
roughness toward me, on learning, as they soon did, that I
was not the wild beast which your treatment inferred me to
be. I owe it to them to say, that they became as civil and
kindly to me as they dared to be. Nor must I omit that Chaplain Jarvis, of the First Connecticut Heavy Artillery, hearing
of the plight I was in, sought me out, and did me many kind-
nesses, often visiting me while I was "sick and in prison," and
bringing not only material supplies, but the far dearer com-
forts of fraternal counsel and support. In the latter part of
my confinement, Chaplain De Forest also, of the Eleventh
Connecticut, was very attentive to me, and, though not nomi-
nally of the same house with me, was just as good as if he
had been ; a true friend and brother indeed.

As for the seasonable relief that came from my old comrades, perhaps I owe you something, Sir, for permitting it. If
so, I thank you, yes, heartily. For it is not at all extravagant
to say, that I should unquestionably have died in a very short
time, at the rate you were going on with me. And the conviction was certainly very strong in me at the time, nor has it
worn out of me yet, that you meant to kill me, provided you
could do so without *seeming* to mean it.

If such was your scheme, it was made impracticable by
that timely intervention ; at least it could not then be put
through with the secrecy which such schemes commonly re-
quire. And whenever I remonstrated with your subordinates
for their harshness to me, they still pleaded that they were but
executing your orders, and that by doing otherwise they would
only get themselves into trouble, without helping me. Moreover, you took good care to let them know that you were my
personal enemy ; and so they understood, of course, that in

persecuting me they were sure of recommending themselves to you, however you might pretend to disown their acts.

The event proved that your purpose respecting me was not substantially changed. I was held under the closest guard, not even being allowed to answer the calls of nature without an armed soldier standing over me ; whether to shield me from invasion, or to keep me from running away, I could not tell. I was also debarred free correspondence with family and friends, my letters being required to undergo revisal by yourself or your deputies. This was indeed a mean and cruel deprivation, and I felt it as such, having never before heard of its being done in case of an officer in arrest. I was told that any letters I might send in unsealed would either be forwarded to their address or returned to me; but I now know that faith was not kept with me in that. And I was shut up in the same narrow inclosure, known as your " bull-pen," along with rebel prisoners, negroes, and the offscourings of your army,—a most lousy, lewd, profane, and ribald set, whose speech was constantly teeming with stuff too bad for any civilized hearing. Their dialect, steeped as it was in filth and crime, might have been pleasing to you, Sir, for it was something like yours ; but it was not pleasing to me. Therewithal, I was in continual dread of catching from them the loathsome vermin ; in fact, it was not possible to avoid doing so. The thought of having my lean body thus made a pasture for Southern live-stock was indeed none of the pleasantest, but I digested it as I best could. And " the familiar beast to man " did not pick my old bones quite bare ; I still have a little flesh and some heart left, notwithstanding your mean and miserable oppressions.

For it hardly need be said that this whole thing was new and strange to me. I had seen many officers of the army in arrest, but I had never before known of any being subjected to such hardships and indignities as these. At the close of our interview, I asked you to let me go in arrest among my own regiment, and there be confined to my quarters ; as in all my experience with the army had been the uniform custom in such cases. You refused. I made the same request again in my written statement to you. Still you refused. One would think my official character and infirm health might have won me that indulgence, even if it had not been customary. Without asserting any peculiar claims to consideration, I may justly ask why you thus excepted me from the honourable usages of the service? Did you find any special motives to roughness in my gray hairs, my recent affliction, and my sacred office? What hindered you from granting my reasonable request? Nothing, evidently nothing, but the mean pleasure you felt in tormenting me, and in putting gratuitous and singular indignities upon me. You had been certified of my age, my ill-health, my studious habits, and the late death in my family. What possessed you thus to trample on my infirmities and my sorrows?

You, my General, were punishing me as a condemned man, yet I had not been tried. For, to officers, the provost-guard prison, even in its best form, is emphatically a place of punishment, and is never regarded as any thing else. You had, and you knew it, a strong personal animosity, a sort of idiomatic virulence, against me; you said you meant to be just, though you scorned to be thought kind-hearted; yet you did not scruple to speak as my accuser, to act as my judge in the very matter whereof you accused, and then to punish me on your own judgment. Where was your respect for even the commonest decencies of justice in that? On putting me in arrest, you told me I was to be tried by my peers. To this I neither spoke nor felt any objections; such a course would have been fair; and I should have had no right to complain of it. For some time I hoped that so it would be. But I knew the law made it your duty to see that, within eight days after my arrest, a copy of the charges, whereon I was to be tried, should be served upon me. Many long, weary weeks passed, still no written charges appeared against me. Meanwhile, you kept me a close prisoner; you victimized me with peculiar severities and dishonours; you held me in a state of debasement unknown to the service: in short, as if anticipating a verdict of acquittal in case I should be tried, and as if determined to make sure of your revenge at all events, you spent all that time in executing upon me the penalties which your own virulence had prompted. Such was your practical commentary on the lawless threat uttered during our interview : "I have you in my power now, sir, and I am going to punish you." Yet you "mean to be just!" You are indeed an original man. May your imitators be few! Up to the time of our interview, I had sharply resented the Southern doctrine respecting you. Will any one blame me if I accept it now?

To relieve the monotony of this review, I will here interpose a brief passage from another hand. On the 24th of September, I applied to you, in writing, for leave to hold religious services in the prison the next day; Sunday, the 25th, being the day on which the President had requested to have special thanksgivings offered in the churches for the recent successes of the national arms. In the course of the day, the application came back to me with the following indorsement :

"RESPECTFULLY RETURNED.—By military usage, an officer under arrest on charges cannot exercise any of the duties of his office. Such permission would be a virtual release from arrest. That your functions are of a high and sacred nature, should have made you more careful in getting under arrest for absence without leave; the penalty of which is Reduction to the Ranks.   (Signed)   "BENJ. F. BUTLER,
                     "Major-General Commanding."

I was aware, my General, of the usage which you here enforced, as I also was of other usages which you so flagrantly disregarded in my case; and I made the request, not in the character of a chaplain, but in that of a Christian minister. This was obvious on the face of it. I was not so green as to suppose myself the chaplain of your bull-pen. I was sorry afterwards that I did not hold the services without asking your leave, and then let you punish me if you would. Anxiety not to offend you was what caused me to do as I did. I confess your refusal grieved me; I did not expect it.

However, the thing had the effect of drawing some part of your fire. I now, for the first time, had authentic notice that I was "under arrest on charges for absence without leave." But I *took* notice of somewhat more than this: it was now plain that you *dared* not allege any other reason for the unlawful course you were taking with me. And I was perfectly

sure you knew my absence without leave to be attended with
such strong mitigations, that no fair-minded court-martial
would convict me of a punishable offence in that matter.
What, then, was it that you here came to me with in your
right hand? I knew that the cause thus alleged was not the
real cause of your proceedings, and that you would have alleged the real one, if you had dared to do so. Indeed, my
General, you overshot yourself in that " pious effusion."
From that time forward I understood the meaning of all you
said about having me tried.

I was now notified, further, that the penalty in my case
was " reduction to the ranks ;" and I understood you as
threatening me with that penalty. In this, it strikes me that
you prevaricated the law somewhat ; that is, you Butlerized
it, or, which is the same thing, looked upon it asquint. The
fourth Article of War reads thus : " Every chaplain commission-
ed in the army or armies of the United States, who shall absent himself from the duties assigned him, (except in cases of
sickness or leave of absence,) shall, on conviction thereof before a court-martial, be fined not exceeding one month's pay,
besides the loss of his pay during his absence ; or be dis-
charged, as the said court-martial shall judge proper." I am
not ignorant, Sir, of the later Act of Congress, which provides that courts-martial shall have power to sentence officers
to reduction to the ranks for absence without leave. But
neither this Act nor any other *prescribes* that penalty for that
offence. It is true, then, that reduction to the ranks *may be*,
but not true that it *is*, the penalty in cases like mine. But
perhaps you meant that I was obnoxious to the penalty in
question, not by the law, but by the exercise of arbitrary
power in breaking the law. If so, you are welcome to all the
truth there was in your unprincipled menace. I had no fear,
though, of your executing that threat upon me. I saw it was
a mere piece of make-believe, and therefore did not believe it.
Be assured, Sir, that the obliquity and indirection fetched from
your late haunts of pot-house litigation and politics will not
stand the fire of military life. Your old " tricks of the trade,"
however they might pass with the " boys" who were wont to
crowd your theatre for the fun of seeing you roast witnesses

in smutty cases, are out of place in the army. He that would deceive must have at least some spice of honesty in him. Notwithstanding your long practice as a moral Harlequin, your playing of the part is too raw and clumsy for any place but the ring; let alone, that you have something to learn, and much to unlearn, before you will be fit for any but ring-men to know.

I had been in your bull-pen four or five days, when Colonel Serrell came to me, and said he had been having a long talk with you about me. That you disclaimed all hard feelings towards me; had no wish to injure me; desired to save me from a court-martial. That you thought I had better write out for you a statement of my case, covering the main points which had come up in our interview; as this might open the way for a settlement without a trial. That if a trial were had, it would be mainly with a view to bring out what I knew about General Gillmore; and you advised me, in that case, to plead guilty to all the charges and specifications, as I would fare better by doing so than by attempting any defence. That, as for my absence without leave, you did not consider this, in the circumstances, any great offence; while the fact of my having been all along a known and allowed correspond-ent of the Press left you little cause against me on that score. I was nothing at a loss, my General, as to the meaning of all this. It was merely the old game of the accuser turning tempter. I saw the trap, however, too plainly to be greedy of the bait.

On the other hand, the Colonel instructed me that you had a perfect right, without a trial, to reduce me to the ranks for absence without leave; and that, in fact, there was no law to restrain you from doing with me any thing you might choose. And he appeared stuck fast in the belief—perhaps you can tell who stuck him there—that, to use his own phrase, you "had got the whip-hand of every body;" insomuch that neither the Lieutenant-General, nor the Secretary of War, nor even the President, dared to thwart or oppose you in any thing. Such was the upshot of his counsel on that head. I well remember how, in answer to something that was said touching the President and you, he spoke of "some men being made to see things through other men's eyes." Did not you plant some such wisdom in him, Sir? or was it the harvest of his own sagacity? Howbeit, the plain inference from all this was, that I stood entirely at your mercy; that no man would dare to help me against you; and that my only refuge from whatever punishments you might please to inflict was by satisfying you, and so making you my friend. The thing, I grant you, was not much, coming, as it did, from a star-hunting coxcomb; it was only a vapid, unsinewed attempt at subornation of false testimony!

The Colonel therefore advised—whether from you or from himself I cannot say—that my best way was "to come out" in my Statement, "and make a clean breast of it"—those were his words—in regard to General Gillmore. This was indeed a rather pregnant hint that you were imputing to me some mysterious knowledge about General Gillmore, which must needs foul my breast with guilt; and that here was a capital chance to cleanse my breast by emptying its foulness into your ears. I had only to make you my father-confessor, and whisper myself out of your clutches by whispering another man in. Wasn't it lovely?

I think, then, I was not far wrong in understanding the Colonel as conveying from you to me both an invitation and a threat: an invitation to damn my soul in order to gratify your malice against General Gillmore, which would engage you to stand my good friend; a threat that, if I failed to do this, you would take measures for roasting that imputed knowledge out of me. I assured the Colonel that you were imputing to me some knowledge about General Gillmore which I really did not possess; that I knew nothing whatever which would answer the purpose of criminating that gentleman; and that I did not see how I could possibly make any statement that would satisfy you, as you evidently wanted something from me which I had not to give. "Do you mean, Colonel," said I, "that General Butler wants me to lie against Gillmore?" "O! no," was his reply; "he only wants you to tell the truth." "But, Colonel, what you say looks very much as though his plan were to wring out of me such truth as he chooses to impute to me. And so, in old times, when the engines of torture were used, it was claimed to be done in order to make the victims tell the truth." This touched his satirical vein, and he replied: "That, I think, Chaplain, was always done by zealous members of the true Church." "It may be so," said I; "but then, you know, General Butler is a remarkably pious man."

On the whole, it was manifest enough that you, my General, had soaked the little Colonel all up. Well, he had been soaked up in like sort divers times before, the process of un-soaking and resoaking him not being a difficult one. For men like him are to men in your place very much what water is to a sponge: it is but to squeeze the sponge, and out comes the water, perhaps bringing away a little of the absorbent's dirt, perhaps leaving a little of its own dirt behind. If you catch the ship sinking, and him staying in it, then you may know he is not a rat.

In all this business, Colonel Serrell was acting—whether consciously or blindly, I am not clear—as your decoy; the programme being, to scare or wheedle, to bully or bribe, to oppress or corrupt me into "bearing false witness against my neighbour." And you were pretending to believe that I had some great secrets locked up in my breast, which, if I could be induced to give them up, would bring General Gillmore fairly under your teeth. I say, you were *pretending;* for, as touching the matter you were in quest of, I had, in our inter-view, told you the truth, and you knew it; my own word, General Gillmore's word, and all the likelihoods of the case converging to the same point. I strongly suspected your game at the time; and what afterwards took place made it clear, that this was indeed the true hinge of your proceed-ings,—namely, to punish me unlawfully for absence without leave, unless I would, by lying and false accusing, enable you to reach and punish another. In the light of such a purpose, your actual treatment of me stood explained; otherwise, it seemed inexplicable. And, as I really had no secrets of the kind to give up, I had little hope of my Statement's working any thing for my relief. For, if General Gillmore had been using me against you, I was not aware of it; and I was quite sure that, if he had meant thus to use me, he would not have been so shallow as to tell me of it. And as I had not knowingly been used by him against you, so I was resolved that, God helping me, I would not knowingly be used by you against him, otherwise than as integrity to God and to my own conscience would allow.

Nevertheless, I set about writing the Statement, taking care to make it as conciliating to you as I could without sinning against the truth. I sent it to you, my General, with much misgiving. For, to satisfy you was out of the question,—God shield me, Sir, from being base enough to catch at such a bait as you threw out to me!—and there remained the alternative of being held in torture by you indefinitely, in the hope of extorting something further from me. I *knew*—for indeed you made no secret of it—that you had two revenges, a greater and a less : I *suspected* that I was to be the victim of the one or the other; that if I could not be made an instrument of the greater, I was to be used as aliment of the less ; so that, in either case, my flesh, " if it would feed nothing else, would feed your revenge." As for General Gillmore, I now had it in full assurance, that, " if you could catch him once upon the hip, you would feed fat the ancient grudge you bore him," for declining to father your military blunders, or to let you shift off upon him the blame and disgrace of them. And so, in this snug arrangement of yours, any one with half an eye might see that Gillmore was to be your real game, I your candle for hunting it ; and that, whether the game were caught or not, the candle was sure to be burned.

In the mean time, my absence without leave was to be worked by you merely as a pretence to cover the deeper scheme in question. Was it not so, my General? You know it was, Sir, and you need not attempt to deny it. In our interview, you told me once that I lied : perhaps you thought so. Did you suppose that if I had lied to offend you, I would much more lie to propitiate you? Nay, Sir ; if I ever hire myself to that branch of the devil's service, it will be under a better tactician than you. You quack it for Satan too clumsily, you mechanize falsehood and prevarication much too coarsely, for my taste. Your style of knavery is too untempered, too exultant, too *immodest*, to please the judicious:

the knave that wins me to strike hands with him in the business must exercise his art with more of the modesty of an artist. If you take this as my reason for preferring General Gillmore to you, I care not; and, my word for it, he will care as little as I. This by the way. You knew of my shattered health, the severe illness of my wife, and my late domestic bereavement. Did you construe all this as a pledge and assurance of an easier and quicker process in subduing me to your purpose? So it would seem from the course you took with me. Because time and disease and sorrow had rendered my blood too thin to yield you much nourishment, therefore, apparently, you craved to suck the more of it. As for any legal adjudication of my case, I now gave up all hope of it. The plain truth was, and is, that you dared not trust your cause to the judgment of a court-martial; and all your talk about having me tried was a mere pretext for keeping me in your bull-pen, and so "punishing" me without a trial. For it soon became evident, that military law and usage were nothing to you, save as you could make them tell against others. The case, I own, seemed to me rather hard; but I knew that so it is apt to be in this world, "when evil men are strong."

Before sending my Statement to you, I made a true and perfect copy of it, which I put into the hands of a tried and faithful friend, together with a note expressing my apprehensions as to the result. I also directed that, in certain contingencies, both the copy and the note should be sent to a particular address in New-York, to be used by my friends there as they might judge best for my defence and protection. In due time, they were so sent and so used, though not used with any decisive effect, till after much bitter proof had come to me, that in taking such precautions I had acted well. The last I heard of the said copy, it had been left in the hands of the Secretary of War. As to the bearing of my Statement in respect of General Gillmore, are you aware what it was, Sir? You tried to roast out of me a crimination of that officer. I gave you—what do you think, Sir?—I gave you a vindication of him. Bless you, my General! I did not mean it; I never once thought of such a thing: I only meant to tell the simple truth; and such, as I have cause to know, was the effect of the simple truth in that case.

My apprehensions proved but too well grounded. Week after week passed away, still no charges were made against me, and I was held there to die, inch by inch, in your bull-pen; as, but for the intervention of friends in New-York and elsewhere, I doubtless should have been held till this time, provided I had lived so long. Meanwhile, Colonel Serrell wrote me several notes, showing a lively interest in my behalf, inquiring whether any progress had been made in my case, and saying you had promised to take it up and dispose of it. I know not whether you were sincere in those promises; but I know that they were not kept, and that the only effect of them was, to press home upon me that experience of hope deferred which maketh the heart sick. And I think it hardly worth the while to speak of sincerity when any act of yours is in question; for, as you have shown yourself to me, there is no truth in you, Sir, nor any thing to build a trust upon. Probably I did not at the time rightly divine the purpose of those friendly notes. I am now of the opinion that they were meant as *feelers*, in order to ascertain whether I was yet ready to give up those wicked secrets which you imputed to me.

At this time, I remained in your old bull-pen, where the number of prisoners had been gradually reduced to a few, and those pretty decent men. But an order now came for removing us up to your new bull-pen, some six miles distant. In the act of removal, I was obliged, lame and feeble and faint as I was, to foot it all the way; the officer in command utterly refusing to let me ride, though there was room in the wagon for half-a-dozen men, and alleging that his orders would not allow it.

Your old bull-pen was, in all conscience, bad enough, but the new one proved, as I anticipated, far worse: the inclosure being much smaller, and crowded with men of the worst description; the ground, too, being so level, that it was impossible to keep my quarters from being flooded whenever there was any considerable fall of rain. Therewithal, it was an uncleaned stable, the beasts having lately been taken out, to

3

make room for us men ; such a place, in fact, as, at that season, no good farmer would think of keeping his cattle in. True, it was within a stone's throw of your own quarters ; and so is a man's pig-pen commonly within a stone's throw of his house. It was inhuman in you, Sir, to keep any thing wearing the human form in that nasty hole. Vile and stupid as many of them were, I pitied, with all my heart I pitied the poor creatures there huddled together, wading and wallowing in the mud and filth from which they could not escape. Physically, most of them were in a worse plight than myself, though probably none of them felt it as I did, there being no personal malice or vindictiveness, and therefore no sense of it, in their case. Besides, the others were, for the most part, confined only for a short time, few of them staying more than a week ; whereas I was kept from week to week, and even from month to month. I remember but two or three who were held through the whole period of my confinement ; and these were young men, healthy, vigorous, and more or less inured to similar hardships and exposures ; all which was not true in my case, and you, Sir, knew it was not. At length, on the 6th of November, you being then in New-York, all the prisoners but myself were taken out of that loathsome inclosure, and removed to Bermuda Hundred. It was an act of great kindness in Colonel Smith, your Assistant Adjutant-General, to except me from that removal ; as the others were now placed in a condition still worse, some fifty being, as I afterwards learned, cooped up in a room not more than eighteen feet square. Of course, had you been at hand, either I should have gone with them, or they would have stayed with me.

Such, my General, is the honest story of your dealings with me. And, however you may "with unbashful forehead" braze it out, I found no small satisfaction in the assurance, which was not wanting, that your treatment of me, so far as it was known in the army, was regarded as "an outrage." For every step of your proceedings in my case was in direct and palpable violation of the law. The 77th Article of War prescribes that, "Whenever any officer shall be charged with a crime, he shall be arrested, and confined in his barracks, quarters, or tent." You confined me in your provost-guard prison, a place such as I have described it to be. The 79th Article of War declares, "No officer or soldier, who shall be put in arrest, shall continue in confinement more than eight days, or until such time as a court-martial can be assembled." You kept me in close prison fifty-three days.

Thus it soon appeared that you cared nothing for the law as contained in the Articles of War ; or rather, that your malice against me was to you a higher law than those Articles, which, be it observed, we all have to subscribe on entering the service. And yet one of the first paragraphs in the Army Regulations declares, " Punishments shall be strictly conformable to military law." Nevertheless, I still hoped for some time, (" the miserable have no other food but hope,") that you would respect the recent Act of Congress, which was passed with a special view to cases like mine, and which made it unlawful for you to keep me in arrest more than forty-eight days. The forty-eight days were passed, still I heard of no release. So, it was clear, that even the solemn enactments of the highest law-making power in the land had no strength or virtue to rescue me from your strange unbenevolence.

You, Sir, had no right to put me in the provost-guard prison at all ; no right to keep me in close confinement anywhere more than eight days ; no right to hold me in any sort of arrest more than forty-eight days ; the settled usage of the army interprets the time to forty days : that is, you had just as much right to shoot, or hang, or starve me to death, as to do what you did. Every provision of law bearing on my case was broken by you. And as week after week passed away, it became more and more evident that I had nothing to hope for in the shape of legal protection. For I was right well assured, that any appeal to the law, any word of remonstrance, any movement for legal remedy or redress, would only be construed by you as a fresh offence, and visited with a further severity. Such was your scheme of "justice." You, Sir, were simply rioting in the abuse of military power, spurning alike at the restraints of law, and the usages of humanity. I never imagined before what it is for an honest man to find himself stripped of all legal protection, and held in the condition of an outlaw. Indeed, Sir, no language of mine can fairly express how much I suffered during those long, dreary, dismal weeks spent in your bull-pen; though far less, to be sure, in the way of physical discomfort, than of mental distress. May God defend you and yours, Sir, from ever suffering what I suffered there, under your hard-hearted and unlawful inflictions! I seemed to be left alone and helpless in the hands of a most unfeeling and vindictive man; that man had discovered himself my personal enemy; he was armed with military power; he was capable of any outrage; there was no sense of honour, no grace of manhood in him; to be mean was his pride, to be brutal his pleasure; he was revelling in the license of assumed impunity; he allowed no law, nor any thing else, to stand between me and his malice. But, much as I suffered · from you, and bitter as is the remembrance of your inflictions, I shall not regret them, nay, I shall take comfort of them, provided your brutal savageness, as exercised on me, should work something towards inducing the country to scour you out of her honourable service.

It may be well to cite, here, an instance or two as showing what a "just man" you are, to make one law for yourself, and another for those in your power. In the course of our interview, you demanded to see General Gillmore's order sending me to New-York on special duty. On my handing it to you, you said it was an illegal order, and I had no right to obey it. I assured you that I was ignorant of that, and had never so much as suspected it; whereupon you gave me to understand that such ignorance would have no force to save me from punishment. This, no doubt, was what you and a certain strutting pronoun of yours meant by the charge of being "absent without proper authority." Some time after my release, I asked Captain Watson whether he was aware that he had been executing illegal orders on me. O yes! he knew it perfectly, he said. I then told him that I had your authority for saying he had no right to obey those orders, and quoted what you had said in reference to General Gillmore's order to me. He replied that he could not help himself, and he would like to see the officer under you that should dare to question the legality of your orders. "But," said I, "you might at least protest against executing orders which you know to be illegal." Yes, he could do that, he said, but it would only get him into the bull-pen. "Well, suppose it should; would you not rather go in there and be a man, than stay out and be something else?" "Oh! I don't want to be in there; any thing but that!" was his reply. I have since learned from the worthy Captain, that he never had any written order in my case, and that he acted all the while under the verbal orders of your immediate sub-altern, Davenport. So! here was another of the Articles of War violated every day that I was kept in prison. But what boots it to speak of those Articles in connection with you? as if your lawless spirit would condescend to know them, save as you might find your pleasure or your pride in breaking them. For it is notorious throughout the army, that your action re-spects the law as little as your speech does the truth; which reminds me of what I have heard as coming from one of our distinguished generals, who knows you well: "No man who respects himself will think it worth his while to contradict any thing that General Butler may say." But I trust, nay, I am sure, it is not in the heart or the head of our Government to sanction or even to tolerate such demoralizing practices in the high places of the military service. You will have to learn more of obedience, Sir, before you can command an army to any purpose but that of undisciplining it.

Again: After I had been in the bull-pen about two weeks, a man was brought there, dressed as a citizen, his leg heavily jewelled with a ball and chain. His name was said to be Cazauran; very likely you may remember him. He was by birth a Frenchman; intelligent, well-spoken, well-mannered, and of some literary acquirement. Withal, he showed con-siderable expertness as a short-hand writer; and I learned that at one time he was employed at your headquarters as a sort of clerk and a reporter for the military courts. That for some cause or other, or on some pretext or other, you had snapped him up, and, without any form of trial, had sentenced him to wear the ball and chain, and to serve sixty days in the outermost rifle-pits of your line. That there you had kept him all that time, right in "the forefront of the hottest battle," the ball and chain still on him. That, soon after he was put there, your newspaper spout at Norfolk published an editorial, endeavouring to blast him with I know not what evil reports, and expressing a hope that "some honest rebel" would shoot him to death. That he had managed to hold up his jewel so as to be seen by the rebels, after which they religiously abstained from firing anywhere near him ; while the soldiers about him had so much pity on him that they would make a sort of hurdle with their muskets, and carry him to and fro between his rifle-pit and his quarters. He told me that he had a family living in St. Louis, and that ever since the date of your sentence he had not been allowed to write or receive any letter whatever. When I first saw him, he had just returned from serving out his sixty days ; he was then kept in the bull-pen some two weeks longer, still wearing the ball and chain ; and was at last sent over the lines into the enemy's territory. What your charges against him were, I had no means of ascertaining : his principal crime was said to be, that he knew too much, or was suspected of knowing too much, about the large contraband trade which certain patriots of yours were carrying on across your lines down in North-Carolina.

Now, my General, taking all the parts together, I really think this was one of the most inhuman things that I ever heard of. I did not meddle with the poor man's antecedents ; he may have been all that you and your creatures gave him out ; I know not, I care not what he had been or what he had done ; nothing could justify the inexpressible cruelty of your proceedings : the veriest fiend that ever made sport of human sufferings, it seems to me, must have relented at the thought of inflicting such protracted tortures. You could not possibly make out so bad a case against him, as I believe he had against you. I know of no justice *here*, that can whip your crime as it deserves.

During your absence in New-York, General Terry, as the ranking officer under you, was left in command. Not knowing how far his authority might reach, but knowing him to be as unlike you in humanity as in soldiership, I wrote to his headquarters as follows :

"PROVOST-GUARD PRISON, HEADQUARTERS ⎱
DEPARTMENT VA. AND N. C., Nov. 8, 1864. ⎰

"*To Captain Adrian Terry, A. A. General, &c.:*

"CAPTAIN : I have now been under arrest, and kept a close prisoner in the provost-guard prison, *fifty* days. My imprisonment has been attended with very extraordinary circumstances of hardship and indignity. I am old and out of health, and ought not to be treated in this way. Soon after my arrest, I learned from General Butler that I was 'under arrest on charges for absence without leave;' still no charges have in legal form been brought against me.

"The law is very clear and positive, that in case of any officer thus under arrest, the arrest shall cease at the end of *forty-eight* days. As an officer of the army, I believe I have the right to know, and I hereby respectfully ask to be informed, for what reasons, and by what authority, the law is thus violated in my case.

"Whatever be the answer to this question, I claim the protection of the law, and solemnly protest against this infraction of it. Respectfully yours, &c.,

"H. N. HUDSON,
"Chaplain First N. Y. Vol. Engineers."

After waiting two days, and getting no reply to this, I wrote to the same headquarters again :

"GUARD-HOUSE, GENERAL BUTLER'S ⎱
HEADQUARTERS IN THE FIELD, Nov. 10, 1864. ⎰

"*To Lieutenant W. P. Shreeve, A. A. A. General, &c.:*

"LIEUTENANT : On the 19th of September, I was put in arrest by General Butler, and handed over to the custody of his headquarters-guard. From that time till the 8th inst., I was kept shut up in his 'bull-pen' along with rebel prisoners, negroes, and the lowest criminals of our army, their bodies infested with lice, their tongues with the most disgusting lewdness and profanity, such as, without very strong reason, no Christian man ought to be forced to hear. During the latter part of the time, the 'bull-pen' aforesaid was too bad a place for any human beings to be shut up in, having lately been used as a stable, and the ground being covered with the refuse of its former occupants. I have been subjected to the horrors and sufferings of this dreadful place, without a trial or a hearing. I am old, and sick, and afflicted, having lately been touched with a great sorrow, such as none but a parent can understand. My health is suffering seriously from the hardships and exposures thus forced upon me.

" On the 8th inst., I was taken out of the ' bull-pen,' and put into the guard-house, where I am still kept along with a parcel of soldiers who spend a good deal of the time in gambling, and nearly all of it in frightful cursing and swearing. I have no privacy at all ; and such is the noise about me that I can hardly get any sleep ; the terrible shocks and strains which I have lately undergone, having rendered me so weak and nervous, that I need quietness for that indispensable process of nature.

" Now, I protest, solemnly, and in the name of God, against this cruel and wanton infliction of punishment upon me, who, I suppose, have the right, in common with other men, to be presumed innocent, until legally pronounced otherwise.

" I have now been held a close prisoner, and in the endurance of this cruel punishment, *fifty-two* days ; whereas the Act of Congress approved July 17th, 1862, clearly and expressly provides, that in case of any officer thus put under arrest, the arrest shall terminate and cease at the end of *forty-eight* days.

" I believe it is my right, therefore, to demand, and I hereby respectfully do demand, to be released from arrest ; and I solemnly warn the military authorities in command to beware how they persist in thus punishing me, against the law, without a trial or a hearing, and to my great and manifest injury. I am willing and ready, as I have been ever since my arrest, to give my parole of honour to obey strictly all lawful orders, and to answer to any charges that are or may be made against me in due form and process of law.

" I herewith enclose a document which will give you all the information that I have, as to the cause of my arrest and punishment. You will see that the document should be carefully preserved and restored to me.

" Respectfully yours, &c.,   II. N. HUDSON,
" Chaplain First N. Y. Vol. Engineers."

The "document" here referred to was your reply, already quoted, to my application for leave to hold religious services in the prison. Late in the evening of the same day, I received the following:

"HEADQUARTERS ARMY OF THE JAMES,
BEFORE RICHMOND, VA., Nov. 10, 1864.

"*Rev. H. N. Hudson, N. Y. Vol. Engineers:*

"SIR: The Brevet Major-General commanding desires me to acknowledge the reception of your letter relative to your release from arrest, and to inform you in reply that he has no power to act in the premises. He is not in command of the Department, nor even of the whole military force within it; he is simply in temporary command of the troops in the field. General Butler is still in command of the Department, although temporarily absent from it, and is still General Terry's commanding officer. Your arrest was made by the order of General Butler as commanding officer of the Department; and it would be manifestly improper for General Terry, or any one not acting as Department commander, to give any orders in relation to it.

"I am directed also to say, that as soon as Major-General Butler returns your communication shall be laid before him.

"I have the honour to be, sir, very respectfully, your obedient servant,

(Signed)   "ADRIAN TERRY,
                            "Captain and A. A. General, &c."

I found no fault with the course taken by General Terry; indeed it was plain enough that he could not do more than he did. But I had gained this advantage, that some parts of my case were now brought to his knowledge; and, as I had known him pretty well during nearly my whole term of service, I could have no doubt of his good disposition towards me. And I had never heard of his doing or saying any thing that looked like setting his "personal feelings" above the law.

Meanwhile, my General, certain forces were brought to bear upon you in New-York, which proved stronger with you than the law. I need not tell you what those forces were. Perhaps you found cause to suspect that the prostitution of your public authority to the work of personal vengeance was not exactly what the Government wanted of you. Be that as it may, you wrote instructions to General Terry as follows:

"Will General Terry, commanding Army of the James, give the following special order?

"HEADQUARTERS ARMY OF THE JAMES, }
November 8, 1864. }

"SPECIAL ORDER No. —.

"Chaplain Henry N. Hudson, having remained under arrest for some time, because of the impossibility of convening a court-martial to try him, because of movements in the field, is released from close arrest, and will report to his regiment for duty; but will upon no pretence leave it."

What sort of an honest man were you, Sir, when you wrote that? You alleged " the impossibility of convening a court-martial to try " me, as your reason for having held me in arrest nearly two months. You had held me all that time, not only in arrest, but in close prison; for which, as you well knew, the reason alleged was, in law, just no reason at all. But let that pass. Notwithstanding your "impossibility," you had, during a large part of that very time, a court-martial in session at your headquarters in the field; and, as I happen to know, case after case was tried by it, of persons whose arrest was subsequent to mine. That is, you here alleged what you could not but know to be false; but then you alleged it for the present satisfaction of those who, as you also knew, could not contradict it. Verily, trickery must have become a passion with you, else you would not be caught botching and bungling it with tricks so flimsy and inexpert as these! Again: On the twenty-fourth of September you could not let me hold religious services in the prison, because leave to do any official act would be " a virtual release from arrest." Now, you ordered me on official duty, and still kept me in arrest, though not in " close arrest."

You sent a copy of the forecited instructions to a friend of mine in New-York, appending thereto a curious note, which I must reproduce:

"November 8, 1864.

"STEPHEN P. NASH, ESQ. :

"DEAR SIR : Above you will find copy of order to be issued in the case of Chaplain Hudson. I believe that I am treating him differently from what I should do to another officer, because I fear lest personal feelings should warp my judgment.

(Signed) "Yours, BENJ. F. BUTLER."

I was right glad, my General, to learn that you were sensible you had "personal feelings." I had been sensible of it a good while, I can tell you. Some thought this little effusion rather dark. To me it seemed clear enough. You meant, of course, that if you had been my personal friend, you would have treated me still worse ; that is, you acknowledged malice, and then alleged that very malice as your motive to special leniency. Is it possible you could suppose that so shallow and shameless a pretext would serve ? "This is most fallible, the worm's an odd worm."

General Terry's order, issued in pursuance of your instructions, reached me on the eleventh of November. Though still, apparently, under some sort of arrest, nobody could tell what, I was now free to go among the dear good fellows of my own regiment, with whom I had spent nearly three years in the service of my country ; free, also, to write as I pleased to family and friends. I remained a sort of prisoner in our camp till the fourteenth of December, when I received an order to report in person at the headquarters of the Lieutenant-General ; and, on doing so, I found that the Lieutenant-General had just been informed of my case by some friends of his in Washington. The day of my full deliverance had come at last. You were then off on your Fort Fisher expedition : what you would have done, had you been at your headquarters in the field, I cannot tell. Nor did I greatly concern myself as to what you might do on your return ; for I was now under the protection of a Soldier and a Gentleman, who was also your official superior, and who, as I well knew, had before rescued officers from your tyrannical and lawless proceedings.

On the seventh of November, you promised my friends in New-York that you would "have me tried very soon." You

had no such purpose, Sir. And, as you manifestly had little
cause against *me*, you encouraged them in the belief "that
your object was, to make the testimony, which you hoped to
elicit in my trial, bear against General Gillmore." Pshaw,
Sir! you knew well enough that such a process would be far
more apt to bring out matter against yourself than against
him. But your promise was thoroughly falsified in that seven
weeks more passed, still I heard of no charges against me,
nor any thing done in preparation for my trial. Where had
you been such a spendthrift of truth, Sir, as to become thus
bankrupt of that treasure? When Colonel Serrell came to
exercise upon me as your decoy, he told me that you dared
not trust yourself to appoint the court and revise the sentence
in my case, because you were conscious of certain infirmities
that might sway you from the line of strict impartiality;
and therefore you proposed referring that matter to the President or the Lieutenant-General. Of course this was said in
order to make me believe that, from a peculiar sensitiveness of
virtue, you would voluntarily waive your legal right in the
premises, and invoke the action of your military superior;
whereas, in fact, you, as the prosecutor in my case, were expressly restrained by law from acting in the matter, and tied
to the very course which you so piously proposed to take.
More than three months have passed since my arrest, and
still, so far from invoking the action of your military superior,
you have not even broached the subject to him. The simple
truth is, you knew I was anxious to leave the service, and you
had not punished me enough yet for dispraising your generalship: my release from the bull-pen went quite against the
grain with you; to keep me still in your power, where I could
not help myself, nor feel secure against further outbreaks of
your vindictiveness, though not all the "justice" which you
craved to inflict, was better than nothing; and so your scheme
was, to hold me there on the pretext that I was to be tried,
and at the same time to devise pretexts for putting off the trial,
that so you might still hold me.

Before quitting this part of the subject, I must relate a little
incident as illustrating rarely well the spirit which animated
you and your sequels, throughout this business. The second

day of my confinement, while I was yet in the magazine-tent, I wrote a brief note in pencil to General Terry, telling him I was there " sick and in prison," with no one to help me or counsel me, and begging the favour of a few moments' interview. I sent the note, open, to the officer in charge, under the promise that any thing so sent should either go to the address, or be returned. The note did not come back, nor did I hear from the General. A few days later, when Colonel Serrell came to practise his peculiar style of Christianity upon me, I spoke of this note, and asked if he knew whether it had gone as directed. He told me General Terry had received it; that he had himself talked with the General about it, who said he could do nothing for me, and had no time to see me. I thought this was not like General Terry; and it seemed right hard that, in my distress, he should thus give me the cold shoulder; for I had but requested an act of charity, and this, too, in a form which no Christian gentleman, such as I held him to be, could well resist. His answer, as reported, hurt me much; however, I swallowed my grief as well as I could; for, notwithstanding my long experience of the Colonel, I dared not think him capable of playing me false in such matter as that. Some weeks after you let me out of the bull-pen, I saw General Terry, and inquired about that note. The thing was now explained; he never saw the note, and knew nothing of it. He did, indeed, see the Colonel, who told him I was in arrest, but left him to suppose me in arrest merely according to law and the settled usage of the army in such cases; and he had no knowledge of my real condition till after you went to New-York. Was Colonel Serrell acting as your chief engineer, Sir, in that business? Howbeit, you and he may arrange between you for the honour of that precious little feat of manhood.

Well, my General, the sum of the whole matter warrants, I think, a pretty grave charge against you. As I have already said, you were my accuser and my personal enemy; I understand you as having admitted the personal enmity in your forecited note to my friend Mr. Nash. As a lawyer, you could scarcely be ignorant of the great legal maxim, that " No man is a good judge in his own case." Yet you presumed to

act as my judge; and then, on your own judgment, without
a trial or a hearing, you dared to punish me with very great
severity for nearly two months; singling me out and excepting
me from the protection of the law, and from the honourable
usages of the service; subjecting me to the most degrading
conditions and associations; utterly ignoring my military rank,
my sacred office, my good name, my faithful service, my years,
my ill-health, and my recent affliction; treating me, in fact,
as an outlaw, and as having no rights which you were bound
to respect. All this, I affirm, was done by you mainly with
the intent to distress and wring me into "bearing false witness
against my neighbour." Moreover, to enforce this wrong upon
me, you took a mean advantage of the military power with
which the Government had clothed you, thus perverting a
solemn public trust to the ends of private malice. Such, Sir,
is my charge. You will meet it as you can.

But I have not done with you yet. The foregoing matter
contains several allusions which, as they stand, are a little ob-
scure; so that I must add something further, to clear them up.
Moreover, one of your motives for wishing to keep me in your
clutches was, you knew right well that I had full and authentic knowledge of certain facts, which facts you desired by all
means to suppress. Indeed, the hope of disabling my testimony in that matter was perhaps the main-spring of your ef-
forts to get from me a lying accusation of General Gillmore.
As I now have you on trial, the occasion must be used for
bringing out those facts.

At our interview, you tried to make me say that General
Gillmore gave me the matter of my letter to Mr. Godwin.
This I could not say, because it was not true. I told you that
General Gillmore did not give me any of that matter; that he
knew nothing of the letter, and I had no speech with him on
the subject of it, till after it was written and mailed. I told
you the same again in my written Statement. I now affirm it
to you once more. And the same, in effect, as I now know,
had been told you twice by the General himself, in the official
correspondence that passed between you soon after the letter
was published. On your demanding who then did give me

the matter, I told you it was given me by Colonel Serrell and other officers of our regiment. I did this with reluctance, but you were pushing me hard, and browbeating me savagely. I now tell you, further, that the whole of that matter—every word, every particle, except my own reflections—was given me by the Colonel himself; though some parts of what he told me were more or less confirmed by other of our officers.

The truth of the affair, as far as I can now recollect it, is just this:

On Tuesday, the seventeenth of May, Colonel Serrell (for you must know, Sir, he had not then got de-sponged from General Gillmore) gave me a long account of what had taken place up at the front during the three or four days preceding. He did this voluntarily, and, as I thought, in the expectation or hope that I would use the matter in my newspaper correspondence; for he had often given me matter to be used in that way. Several of our officers then in camp were personally knowing to the fact of the Colonel's giving me the matter in question; and they also understood just as I did his purpose in doing so. On the strength of what he thus told me, I wrote the letter to Mr. Godwin, which, I think, was dated the eighteenth, though, possibly, a day or two later. In the morning of Saturday, the twenty-first, after the letter had gone, I went to the Corps Headquarters to call on the rebel General Walker, who had been wounded and captured the day before. That done, as General Gillmore was in his tent, I then called on him, and said: "General, I want to ask you one question; if it is an improper one, you will know it to be so, and will treat it accordingly." He said he would hear the question. I then asked him, "Did you, after capturing the enemy's line of works up near Drury's Bluff, send Colonel Serrell to General Butler, with a proposal to fortify our position there?" "Yes, I did," said he: "the works needed a little engineering, so as to face the other way." I replied, "That is all, General; I ask no more; for I do not think it fair that I should be pumping matter out of you." This, to the best of my recollection, was the first speech I had with General Gillmore after he left Hilton Head, and the only speech I had with him till after the letter to Godwin was published.

While General Mitchel was in the Department of the South, on consultation with him I wrote a private letter to Mr. Horace Greeley, with whom I had been slightly acquainted several years. Mr. Greeley politely responded, requesting to hear from me occasionally. I therefore now wrote him a letter also, the same in substance as that to Mr. Godwin. I think this was written after the forecited talk with General Gillmore ; and, if so, I may have stated that the main point of it had been substantially confirmed to me by him.

This, my General, is the whole and simple truth of that proceeding, as far as I now remember it. As Colonel Serrell was my informant, I trust you will allow that the contents of my letter to Mr. Godwin were " derived from an authentic source." For your further delectation, I will next offer you a brief service of retrospect, hoping that you will be able to " read, mark, learn, and inwardly digest " it.

After capturing the enemy's line of works near Drury's Bluff, which, I think, was done on Saturday, the 14th of May, General Gillmore sent Colonel Serrell to you, with verbal instructions to lay before you a plan for shortening the line and facing it towards Richmond ; because the works, having been constructed for defences against us, obviously needed certain changes in order to make them available as defences against the enemy. The General also sent you at the same time, and by the same hand, a written message to this effect : That, in case the enemy should seriously threaten his left, he had not force enough there to occupy the whole of the captured line ; and that, if the extreme left were not occupied, it would be necessary to withdraw beyond range of that position. On receiving the message, you gave this answer : " Say to General Gillmore, we are on the offensive, not defensive ; he need have no apprehension about his left ;" an answer so absurd and infatuate, that I am at a loss how to account for it, but upon the supposal of your having been specially inspired to utter it. Howbeit, the Colonel thereupon returned and reported your wisdom to General Gillmore in the hearing of several officers. I think you will hardly venture to deny that this is a fair and truthful statement of the matter in hand. I leave it to you to settle with the country and with yourself for the strange and dreadful infatuation of your answer to General Gillmore's timely and judicious proposal. Would to God you had met that proposal as wisely as it was made!

Early in the morning of the following Monday — do you not remember it, Sir?—you found the case somewhat altered; you were suddenly put on the defensive; and I suspect it then became apparent even to you, though not till too late, how potent and how prolific was the unwisdom of your fore-cited answer. "Short, sharp, and decisive," as your own saucy smartness, was the discomfiture which then swept over you. For your own sake, I would fain hope that the events of that morning may have chastised some of the airish, braggart self-importance out of you, and reduced your insane conceit nearer to the level of your capacity.

While the fight was in progress, you sent, in rapid succession, first, two verbal orders, and then at least three written ones, to General Gillmore, to leave his position within the enemy's line, and fall back. The first *verbal* order was carried by General Martindale; the second, by an officer of your staff, whom I forbear to name. On receiving the first, General Gillmore went forthwith to making preparations for doing as you ordered. This necessarily occupied some time, for the enemy was pressing him in considerable force, so that he could not move at once without incurring serious loss. Your last *written* order was very peremptory, commanding him to withdraw immediately. By that time his dispositions were completed, and he withdrew in good order, bringing off nearly all his wounded, and also most of his material.

After falling back some half or three-fourths of a mile, General Gillmore took up a good position, and there paused, to cover your retreat. There you came upon him, and called him to account for what he had done. He produced your written orders. These of course you could not deny. But you alleged that he had begun his arrangements for falling back before he received either of those orders. He admitted this, but cited your *verbal* orders as his reason for doing so. You thereupon denied those verbal orders, and proceeded to censure him as having acted without authority, in that he had anticipated your first written order, and begun his preparations

4

for moving before it reached him. What ailed you, Sir, that you undertood to play the soldier in such a garb as that? Were you frightened out of your wits? or did your quickness of wit beguile you into an act which honest men cannot appreciate?

It is not always easy to catch the aims or divine the motives of so intricate and eccentric a moralist as you. Here you had achieved a second blunder in ordering General Gillmore to fall back; he being of the opinion, as others also were, that, apart from your order, there was no necessity for him to budge an inch. And your written orders were avowedly based on information which soon after proved to be false. Those reported successes of the enemy—very important, if true—against General Ames and Colonel Howell in your rear, were, as you presently learned, bogus. It was then apparent to you, no doubt, that with a fair measure of pluck and steadfastness the position, which you had now lost, might have been held; in which case the enemy would soon have been forced to relinquish the advantage he had gained in another part of the field. Your noble courage, which had oozed off so charmingly while the enemy was hot upon you, returned in full blast the moment you had none but your subordinates to deal with. Let me congratulate you, Sir, on having that great heart of yours charged with a bravery so prompt and so wise to temper itself in inverse proportion to the danger. " Why, Hal, thou knowest I am as valiant as Hercules; but beware instinct." Surely it must be fitting and right that such a hero as you should put on his bravest looks, when danger stands at a respectful distance, as fearing to meet him. For the courage that rises in the face of peril, and modestly retires when the peril is past,—what does such a courage argue but a plentiful lack of wit? And so your aim in this case appears to have been to outface General Gillmore, with your redundant valour, into assuming, or at least sharing, the blame of having lost his position within the enemy's line; as though your ordering him to withdraw had been but an after-thought suggested by what you found him already preparing to do. Be that as it may, General Martindale, at the last accounts, was still alive, and was still man enough and soldier enough to bear witness to the truth in this matter; thus fixing upon you the entire responsibility of the movement in question.

Perhaps I ought to add that the line of works which General Gillmore held that morning connected with the system of defences on Drury's Bluff, and extended westward across the Richmond and Petersburgh Railroad. Ten hours well spent in fortifying would have secured your foothold in that most important position. As it was, the evening of that day saw the whole army back within your line of intrenchments. The enemy soon gathered across your front, shut you in, and there held you, so that you could not get out. Within eight-and-forty hours, trains of cars were running over the road which you had so lately controlled, and have been running ever since. It was indeed a bad day for you, my General; bad in more senses than one. For seven long months two armies have been labouring with all their might to retrieve the loss of that memorable day, and have not retrieved it yet.

And here it may not be amiss to spend a thought or two upon your admirable gift of alternate inflation and collapse. For you were evidently blown big with presumption when you refused to fortify, as General Gillmore proposed; and this signal act of rashness was followed, as such acts are apt to be, by a no less signal act of timidity; you being, in the hour of trial, scared into an abandonment of the position which, in the flush of success, you had rashly scorned to strengthen. So "kingdom'd Achilles in commotion rages, and batters down himself." I suppose you find it both convenient and pleasant thus to have your "valiant parts" now distended with arrogance, now crushed together with impotence, inversely to the occasion. But I hope you will forgive us ordinary mortals, warm questrists of amusement as we are, if we indulge now and then in a quiet laugh at this your preposterous style of manhood. Of course your style is right, Sir—at least for you; but this does not hinder it from being a little odd; I have sometimes sinned so far as to think it almost comical. I commend you to the study of Monsieur Parolles. And, as a relish to the contemplation of that noted hero, I will here insert an apt soliloquy of one Captain Bessus,* merely premising that

* A famous character in Beaumont and Fletcher's *King and No King*.

the Captain has just been cowed into surrendering his sword, but is allowed to retain his knife ; whereupon he solaces himself with these audible thoughts : "I will make better use of this than of my sword. A base spirit has this 'vantage of a brave one ; it keeps always at a stay; nothing brings it down, not beating. I remember I promised the king, in a great audience, that I would make my backbiters eat my sword to a knife. How to get another sword I know not ; nor know any means left for me to maintain my credit, but impudence : therefore I will outswear him, and all his followers, that this is all that's left uneaten of my sword."

As to the false information on which you claimed to be acting during the fight of the 16th of May, I know not who gave it, nor what business you had to be thus imposed upon by treacherous or incompetent messengers. I have heard, indeed, that you then had certain Southerners professedly serving you as spies and informers ; and it was thought by some that they stuffed you with those forged alarms for the very purpose of fooling you into doing just what you did. This was told me by a good and true man, who was at that time on duty at your headquarters ; but I cannot vouch for it. I would not wonder if it were true, though ; for, be assured, Sir, none are more easily gulled than they who have got intoxicate with a conceit of shrewdness and sagacity. As you specially plumed yourself on knowing your man, so you might well be a fit subject for the enemy's spies and informers to practise upon. The voracious vanity of Ajax makes him an easy prey to the flatteries of Ulysses : behold him eagerly sucking in the poison that has been craftily qualified to his taste ! You, my General, love the voice of sycophants ; they are your chosen guides ; to beguile you of your trust, they have but to cram you with pleasing falsehoods ; you will taste no treachery in any thing that is sugared over with that disguise ; and so you are well paid for spurning at the reproofs of honest men.

Thus much for your two main blunders in that famous adventure on Proctor's Creek ; which blunders, as described to me soon after by Colonel Serrell, were the whole staple of my letter to Mr. Godwin; though the matter has since been further explained and certified to me by better vouchers. I need not stay to comment on the Colonel's exorbitant virtue in urging me, as he afterwards did, to "come out and make a clean breast of it," by Butlerizing upon another man the very tale which he knew to have been spun into my ears from his own exuberant lips. Doubtless I should have cause to be ashamed, or alarmed, at his daring to do so, but that brass is known to be a rather dull metal. As it is, I console myself with the reflection, that he would not have had the effrontery thus to tamper with me, if he had had the sense to understand me. True, he did it to please you, Sir; but that only argues him fit to be your pimp. What if he should say some time hence, that he would not have tried such arts on me, but that he knew I was proof against them?

Now, you also knew that Colonel Serrell gave me the matter of my letter to Mr. Godwin; for I told you so, plainly, in our interview, and you believed what I said: I read conviction in the lines of your face, as you heard my words. Moreover, General Gillmore, as I have already shown, had told you twice in writing that he did not give me the matter of that letter. So that your proceedings in this case were not for the purpose of getting from me what you believed to be true, but of making me utter what you knew to be false. But I think your "high-erected spirit" must have had rare sport in thus employing Colonel Serrell as your undertaker in the business of inducing me to father his own gift on General Gillmore. A clever stroke of art, my General! if it showed a good deal of knavery, it also showed some wit. Of course you did not tell him what I had told you, nor did I tell him; for, to be frank, I rather enjoyed, as I presume you did, his maiden essays in the Butler craft. But let me assure you that such a gust of sharp practice is not very wise. They who have become fanatics in trickery seldom deceive any but themselves.

From the foregoing account it appears that your deplorable military blundering in the affair under review was not the worst of it. Great as were your mistakes, considerate and kind-hearted men might have overlooked them, had you owned them frankly like a man, and bravely stood up to the re-

sponsibility of them. I grieve to say that the swift reverse
which fell upon you, though it may have taught you something in the art of war, failed to elicit any sparks of honour
and manhood. Nay, more; whatever virtue there may have
been in the lessons of that time to bring forth such fruits "in
an honest and good heart," seems in your case to have fructified in quite another sort. To be sure, the blunders could not
be undone, nor the loss and damage consequent thereon fore-
closed. But here was at least a good chance for you to ac-
quire the honour of nobly acknowledging the fault, though you
could not retrieve it. And I think all right-minded men will
agree that the frank acknowledgment of such a fault is something better as regards the honour of a man, than not to have
committed it. It is thus that truly noble spirits turn adversi-
ties into felicities, losses into glorious gains, the very darkness
of fortune serving to augment and illustrate their virtue. But
it appears that you, instead of earning any such praise, were
kindled just the reverse : either because you were so unmanned
by the events of the day as not to know what you did, or else
from an innate something which I refrain from wording as it
is, you endeavoured to fasten upon him who had counselled
you well the very consequences proceeding from your own
fatal rejection of his counsel. O, my General, what a fall
was that! And you have ever since been seeking to revenge
your blunders on those whose only crime was that of knowing
and lamenting them. From your manner of dealing with me,
one would suppose your huge miscarriage had never happened,
if I had not gone and told of it. Did you imagine that by
punishing me for grieving aloud over your fault you could
really make me guilty, and yourself free ?

As you seemed to be taken with "a strong delusion" about
General Gillmore—such a delusion as often leads men to "believe a lie,"—I am minded to add a few words more touching
the matter between him and you.

I repeat, that if General Gillmore had been forging any
plots, or working any arts against you, I knew nothing of them
whatsoever. You accused me of being in a conspiracy with him.
I submit that if he have the mind of a conspirator, he knows
better than to take a man like me into an enterprise of that

sort. And I owe it to him to say, that I had never heard him speak an unkind or disrespectful word of you. But then, if he had had any such to speak, I was probably one of the last persons in the world that he would have been likely to speak them to. For the little intercourse I had held with him, though amicable enough, had nothing of the confidential in it. And I suspect that gentleman is not much used to "unpacking his heart with words" in denunciation of his official brethren. Be that as it may, I had all along believed you both to be good men and true; and my deepest wish had been, that the best talents and best services of you both might be forthcoming in the great cause of the Nation. But I had lived in the world long enough to know, that good men sometimes misunderstand one another, and so fall at odds. And if it was so with you, that was not my business, nor had I made it my business. I was willing, in my place, to fight with or for either or both of you against the rebels; but I was not willing to fight with or for either of you against the other. You had both, as I thought, done good service in the cause, and I honoured you both for it. And what right had you, my General, to be making war on him, even though you knew ever so well that he had been warring against you? If you could not both walk the same road of duty together, then why not agree to walk apart, and let each other alone? Or, if he would not do this, why not do it yourself nevertheless, and so take the chance of outdoing him in the public service? It really seemed to me that you were both bound, by every just consideration, to spend all your force in the common work, postponing your private quarrels, if you had any, till the rebellion should be thrashed back to —— to where it came from. And I must say, my General, that in my poor judgment the little time and thought you have spent in persecuting me had far better been spent in prosecuting the great war of the Union. Depend upon it, such an use of your powers would have fructified more to your credit.

As for yourself, it is true I did not believe you to be a great general, nor even capable of becoming one. Neither do I believe it now, your campaigning against Richmond and your bull-penning of me having alike failed to convince me of it.

But what of that? there were other and even higher paths of honour open to you, in the just exercise of those administrative talents which you were supposed to possess. On the score of these, I had myself wished all honour to you. My thought and my speech had been : " General Butler is a strong man, a very strong man, and a glorious good fellow, in the right place. He has greatness enough of his own, if he would only be contented with it ; but, in aspiring to another sort of greatness, he will hazard the disappointing of that which is properly his, and at the same time fail of that to which he aspires."

Such, I say, had been my thought and speech ; not very wise indeed, but honest and frank. And if my mind has since changed somewhat respecting you, it is but such a change as experience often superinduces upon minds far stronger and firmer than I can suppose mine to be. I, in common with many others, had accorded to you high administrative abilities. A nearer view of you, aided by the disenchantment which your peculiar manners and your singular perfections as a gentleman are so well adapted to effect, has convinced me that I was mistaken in this ; and that your genius, instead of being properly administrative, is merely of the detective and machinative order. To be a chief of police, or a sort of municipal rat-catcher and wolf-tamer, is, I take it, about the true pitch and scope of your capacity ; unless you may be thought to have a special gift for harrying and buffeting witnesses and chaplains. Not to put too fine a point upon it, you are strangely wanting in the right temper of the administrative faculty : you have nothing of the magnanimity that belongs to that type of mental organization, and you abound in the meanness and petty vindictiveness that do not belong to it. The generous thought, the high principle, the large discourse, the understanding soul,—there is not a gleam of these about you. And I think a man can hardly do well in any office of public administration, unless he have *some* conscience,—enough, at least, to enable him to recognize the workings of conscience in other men, and to appreciate those workings as an operative element in the problems with which he has to deal. Observe, I do not here question but men may be great fools in all this : I merely urge the fact that conscience is an actual force in human affairs; and that some account should be made of this force, if one would go smooth with the existing order and compact of things. Nor must I omit, that you are evidently nothing if not circumventive, and that nature does not like to be circumvented on so large a scale; she may indeed, for a while, humour the lust of stratagem and artifice, but it is only for the sport of seeing "the engineer hoist with his own petar." For we shall see, in the long run, that truth and law are too much for you; they will grind you up; so that the not caring to do right will lose you the power of *doing* any thing. I grant you to be a man of quick, sharp, and ready parts; you have a very considerable gift of practical adroitness, which you seem to mistake for wisdom; your brain is as fertile as an old barn-yard, though its up-growth is neither wholesome nor sweet; even in your best preparations we still find you dabbling in the dirt of vulgar smartness and claptrap; and of your whole style and expression it may be justly said,

"Of courage we see little there,
  But, in its stead, a medley air
  Of cunning and of impudence."

I believe you manage to get more official brain-sprouts before the public, than all the rest of our generals put together; and nearly every one of them has some jerk or snap of Butlerism which is neither wise nor in good taste. These fond and fluent spurts appear to be the orts or old-ends of your long practice at blackguarding and abusing witnesses. They may answer as ear-ticklers for the groundlings and pitmen, before whom you have been used to perform; but they are much too theatrical for a well-ordered stage, and none but third-rate or fourth-rate actors ever affect them. At all events, such issues are not the right style of a solid and symmetrical manhood: an Englishman would be apt to say they smell of the Old Bailey; a sensible American might regard them as doing well enough for a Tombs lawyer, but not just the thing for a general in the field: a Jeffries, a Scroggs, or even an Alsatian Duke Hildebrog, could beat you at them: I suspect we have several generals who could at least equal you in them, if they would let themselves down so low. Besides, you have been performing in that kind long enough: what was at first a rather entertaining exhibition, has got "played out" into an uncomely exposure: the wit, if there be any in it, is of the cheapest sort, and can no longer raise a laugh, save at your own expense: in brief, the thing has grown stale; you had better leave it off.

Such, my General, is the best figure I can make of you. I hope you will recognize the likeness, though of course you cannot be expected to see yourself precisely as others see you. Taking you for all in all, you are now, I should think, the fitting sequel and continuation of what you were when I used to hear a good deal about you as "the hard case of the Lowell Bar;" your changes of character being only such as would naturally grow from having more room to spread yourself in, and less restraint upon your native aptitudes. Men who have conversed much with you in your present full-blown efflorescence, may indeed fear you, may fawn upon you, may wonder at you; but they cannot, they cannot respect you.

And now a word more as to the cause of your resentment against me.

Last May, soon after landing with your army at Bermuda Hundred, you got possession of the railroad between Richmond and Petersburgh, and held it, I think, something over a week. During that time, you might have taken up a position commanding the road, fortified, and made sure of it beyond all reasonable peradventure. This was the wise thing for you to do; but you preferred, apparently, to be doing something more noisy and brilliant. For a while, your movement was successful; success, I take it, elevated you somewhat; and in your elevation you saw some things that were not, and failed to see some things that were. Witness, your unlucky dispatch to the Lieutenant-General, assuring him that you had effectually cut off Beauregard from reinforcing Lee. For you must know, Sir, that giddiness is no good strengthener of the vision for the *seeing of facts as they are;* and that to see facts as they are is of all things the most needful in a commanding general.

Now, I understood at the time, or thought I understood, the importance of holding that railroad. As I have already stat-

ed, on the 16th of May you lost control of the road, lost it
beyond recovery; and this, too, by what I could not choose
but regard as one of the greatest and most inexcusable blunders of the whole war. Indeed, my General, it was a dreadful miscarriage, and the nation has paid dearly for it since,
both in blood and treasure; five hundred millions of dollars
and fifty thousand lives being, probably, but a moderate esti-
mate of the cost thus entailed through the wrong-headed, vain-
glorious conceit and egotism of a general who was no soldier,
overbearing the counsels of a sober and judicious soldiership.
I was certainly led to believe at the time, and did believe, as
indeed I still do, that if the advice of Generals Smith and
Gillmore had been followed, the result would have been very
different. I deplored the miscarriage much: I thought we
had had enough of civilian commanders in the field: I longed,
more than I know how to express, to have our military work
go on in the conduct of educated soldiers, instead of sworded
lawyers. Still I knew right well that in all human affairs,
but especially in war, the best men are liable to make mistakes; that such mistakes may draw on very serious consequences; and that wise men, instead of brooding past mistakes, rather make it a point to remember them only that they
may learn how to go on and do better.

With these thoughts pressing upon me, I wrote the letter to
Mr. Godwin, setting forth the fact and the circumstances of
the miscarriage, as I understood them. The letter, against
my expectations, was published. I was, and I still am, well
assured, that the letter, though erroneous in some of the de-
tails, was in its main points substantially true. But you, I
suppose, were ambitious to be distinguished as a great general,
perhaps as the greatest of all our generals. To have achieved
the capture of Richmond, would have gone far towards making that distinction yours. I impute not such ambition to you
as a fault; on the contrary, I should regard it as a high virtue in you, provided you used none but just and honourable
means to compass your object. But it was obvious enough
that the recent miscarriage would operate as a material draw-
back on your ambition of military renown, in case it should
become generally known to the public. And, through the

letter aforesaid, I became, undesignedly, a means of making it thus known.

This, my General, and nothing but this, was the true motive, the real secret, of your unbenevolent proceedings against me; you knew it was, and you knew, moreover, that I knew it was. Indeed you evidently wished me to understand that such was the case, and to suppose that my only chance of escaping your clutches was by arming you with something wherewith to twist General Gillmore. So that I feel amply warranted to say, that your treatment of me was not for any purpose of military order and discipline, but to the end either of taking vengeance directly on me, or else of inducing me to serve as your instrument of vengeance on another. Whether you acted, also, with the further view of making an example of me as a newspaper correspondent, to the end of reducing other newspaper correspondents to a course of entire subserviency to yourself, that so you might have them to officiate, unreservedly, as your advocates and puffers in the public ear, I pretend not to say. But this I know full well, that correspondents who did what they could to discredit major-generals under you were not put in your bull-pen. And perhaps it was but natural for you to presume, in respect of me, that " your defeat did by your own insinuation grow." Nevertheless, I protest that the fact of others having served as your spouts against General Gillmore, does not necessarily infer me to have been serving as his spout against you.

What, then, my General, had you in all this business to bottom any decent plea of right or even expediency upon? I had but given, in the form of a private letter, a fair and honest statement of what I had fairly and honestly learned touching the matter in question. But suppose I had done this avowedly for publication, with my usual signature, still it was at the worst but a military offence; there was no breach of essential morality in it; nothing to call for any extra-judicial infliction; and therefore it ought not on any account to have been visited beyond the strict requirements of military law: whereas you did nothing but violate the law in my case, and this for the purpose of a severity far greater than the law would award. Do you think, by such ignoble and unmanly abuse of military power, to stifle the honest convictions of men respecting you, or to purchase exemption from the just responsibility of your acts? Who, what, I pray, are you, Sir, that you should take upon you, against the law, and without a trial, to punish men for a candid and liberal expression of judgment about you? This is mere tyranny, Sir, and tyranny of a very bad kind; such as, if unchecked, can hardly fail to quench the life of all true soldiership under you. Nor is mine by any means a solitary case: your military career has notoriously been replete with like instances of arbitrary and unlawful punishment. And what think you has been the effect? to make the men respect you? No, Sir; not a bit of it: it has merely set them to execrating you, or to making fun of you, and venting broad jokes about you. And, as you have been going on, no officer worthy of his title could think his reputation safe with you: all must feel themselves put to the alternative of being at odds with you, or else of becoming your creatures; no way left but to be nothing at all, or be just what you please to have them, mere putty-heads and dough-faces to you; either of which is fatal to the spirit and efficiency of an army. Therefore—I speak advisedly—therefore some of the very best officers in your command have withdrawn from the service, or have asked to be relieved, on the ground that they could not possibly serve under you either with benefit to the cause, or with credit to themselves. And what could we expect, under such a rule as yours, but that the angel of respect and confidence should give place to the demon of hatred and distrust? men meeting each other with chilled looks and staggering eyes; drawing the cloak of suspiciousness tight about them, and moving as though they dared not say their souls were their own; hardly speaking together but in whispers, and constantly on the alert lest some of your prowlers and informers might be eyeing them. Such, my General, is the style of military order and discipline which your genius creates about you. And, instead of that which should accompany your place, " as honour, love, obedience, troops of friends," you have—are you aware of it, Sir?—

"Curses, not loud, but deep, mouth-honour, breath,
Which the poor heart would fain deny, but dare not."

Indeed, Sir, you greatly overween in thinking, as you seem to have done, that this war was gotten up, under Providence, mainly to the end of furnishing you with a world to bustle, and play the autocrat, and promulgate yourself, and air your smartness in. The people of this nation, and even we men of the army, have, or think we have, a higher concern, a more sacred duty, than to push and crouch and wrangle for the privilege of walking about meanly conspicuous betwixt your legs. And some of us, at least, have other work to do besides smoking your blunders and failures out of the public eye. Nor do we reckon it the dearest of honours to be trampled upon even by men much greater than you are. We have no military laurels to spare but for those who earn them by real and solid service to the cause; nor do we hold the cause to be served, when they whose office it is to enforce the laws grow so big in their own esteem, as to take pride in breaking them. But you "had got the whip-hand of every body?" Ah! Sir, that was a mistake; you never had any such thing. Well, my General, you, in the pride and insolence of unaccustomed power—robes which upstarts seldom know how to wear—have been strutting through your brief term of adventitious greatness, apparently not remembering those old maxims, that "a haughty spirit goeth before a fall," and that "the prosperity of fools shall destroy them." Did you, when your sun was high, dream, like the bold bad woman in the play, that there was no need of fear, "since none could call your power to account?" Alas! Sir, that was the very time of all others when you should have given earnest heed to the precept, "Let him that thinketh he standeth take heed lest he fall."

I have said that I had not believed you capable of becoming a great general. But I never had the least objection to your becoming such. On the contrary, if you had soldiered your way to honour and distinction, I should have been right glad of it; most assuredly I should. No one rejoiced at your success more heartily than I did; no one prayed more earnestly that you might still succeed. The capture of Richmond by you would have made me fairly leap for joy. But I question whether your "gentle exercise and proof of arms" on me has greatly furthered your reputation for soldiership. When a man is hunting tigers, he should not turn aside, no, not for an instant, to catch and tease a mouse. Your great campaign on the James in May was not successful. I confess you succeeded better in your little campaign of September on the Hudson ; this exploit being, apparently, just the height of your military genius.

But, my General, permit me to assure you that in this latter enterprise your proceedings, though perhaps not wanting in smartness, were something ill-judged. For, in the first place, the fact of your grand miscarriage could not possibly be smothered up from the world ; the public would have known and appreciated it just the same, though I had never written a word about it. In the second place, it was very evident that the legitimate effect of your course with me would be, to convince the public of the truth of what I had written about you, however they may have doubted it before. It was therefore supremely unwise in you to think of refuting my statements, or of reversing the public judgment, by letting loose your vindictiveness on me. Allow me to remind you, Sir, that " when valour preys on reason, it eats the sword it fights with." That a man of your hardness should do wrong to another, is not so strange. But I marvel that a man of your shrewdness should commit so great a blunder in so small a matter. For I am hugely mistaken, if your treatment of me do not prove more damaging to you, than any thing I had written or could write about you. Just think of it : You had made a fool of yourself in certain military doings ; I had told of your folly ; to be revenged on me for this, you then went and made a fool of yourself a second time. I know not what was the trouble with you : my theory is, that the lawyer prevented the soldier in you, and the straining to be a soldier subverted the lawyer ; so that your mind became as thwart and ill-conditioned as your manners. What you should have resented was your own blundering, not my exposure of it : whatsoever my act or my motive may have been, that was the wise and manly thing for you to do. To "kill your physician, and the fee bestow upon the foul disease," is not the best way, not absolutely the best. Suppose you had crushed my body into the dust ; or, worse, suppose you had crushed my spirit into uttering that about General Gillmore which I knew to be false; what could this have done toward retrieving your miscarriages, or undoing your blunders? or even toward altering the public verdict respecting them? Believe me, there were other and better ways of approving your generalship, than by insulting and browbeating a defenceless chaplain. Let me tell you, Sir, that if you would be distinguished as a general, you will have to do something besides oppressing and tormenting so impotent and so insignificant a being as myself. Shame, shame on you, General Butler! For decency's sake, "assume a virtue, if you have it not."

Sincerely yours, &c.,

H. N. HUDSON.

POSTSCRIPT.

In the foregoing letter I have expressed the conviction, that all the while you held me in your claws it was not your purpose to have me tried ; and that your talk about doing so was a mere pretext for keeping me in your bull-pen, and so punishing me without a trial. This conviction has been rather strengthened than impaired by what has since occurred. On being removed from your late command, as my case was rather prominent among those brought against you, you then turned and made charges against me. I have not yet seen those charges, and know not what they are, though I have looked diligently, and as far as I could, to find a copy of them. It was your business to see that a copy was served on me. That you have not done so, is proof enough, both in law and in reason, that you still did not mean to give me the benefit of a trial.

At the time the charges were made, I was at home on leave of absence by the Lieutenant-General. When my leave was out, which was on the 26th of January, I returned to my regiment, and there have remained till this day, waiting to hear from you. My term of service has now expired. You have had ample time, Sir, for carrying out any honest purpose of a trial ; and I am under no sort of obligation, either in duty or honour, to wait any longer for you. I learn, on good authority, that, though the charges were not made till after your removal, yet you dated them back several days before that event. Of course, this was done to hide the glaring anachronism of your proceedings,—another bald and blear-eyed trick of yours. And it is the opinion of those most competent to judge in the matter, that on being called to account for your criminal treatment of me, you thought it necessary to patch up something, in order to break or parry the force of what was charged upon you. But the thing had then reached a point where such stale and disreputable shifts would not go. It was vain to tinker at your broken cause in that way, but I suppose you must still be false. The power with which you had so long oppressed and insulted me was not incorporate with you ; the meanness was.

In addition to your other heroisms, you are now the hero of Fort Fisher,—a very fitting consummation of your military career. I believe a good deal in the sagacity and wisdom of President Lincoln; and when you were ordered to report at Lowell, I presume it was because he judged that you could serve the country better there than anywhere else. I have read your Lowell speech. Of course I did not fail to observe the freedom with which you there criticised and censured the military doings of the Lieutenant-General. Your virtue is certainly of a very eccentric habit. In that speech, you made no scruple of doing, in the most aggravated and most offensive form, the very thing which you tried to kill me for having done in the most excusable form. I am far from imputing to you any conscience of injustice in this; for, as seen through your eyes, it is, I doubt not, perfectly right and just that you should thus punish to death an ounce of fault in another, and still expect impunity for a ton of the same fault in yourself. But, with such an illustrious example before me, I shall hope to be pardoned for remembering the saying of a very wise man, that "faction is but tyranny out of office."—But you are now a fallen man, and so I forbear ; indeed, I would not have said so much, but that your mean-spirited vindictiveness towards me has manifestly survived your fall.

H. N. H.

Camp First New-York Volunteer Engineers, }
Army of the James, Feb. 13, 1865. }